Lucas's baby.

Tara's fingers crept to [ ]
and she saw him follow the move[ ]
watchful attention of a cheetah she'd once se[ ]
on a TV wildlife program, just before it pounced
on some poor and unsuspecting prey.

"How...pregnant are you?" he questioned, lifting
that empty gaze to her face.

He said the word *pregnant* like someone trying
out a new piece of vocabulary, which was rather
ironic given that he was such a remarkable
linguist. And Tara found herself wanting to tell him
that it felt just as strange for her. That she was
as mixed-up and scared and uncertain about the
future as he must be. But she couldn't admit to
that because she needed to be strong. Strong for
her baby as well as for herself. She wasn't going
to show weakness because she didn't want him to
think she was throwing herself in front of him and
asking for anything he wasn't prepared to give.

One Night With Consequences

When one night...leads to pregnancy!

When succumbing to a night of unbridled desire, it's impossible to think past the morning after!

But with the sheets barely settled, that little blue line appears on the pregnancy test, and it doesn't take long to realize that one night of white-hot passion has turned into a lifetime of consequences!

Only one question remains:

How do you tell a man you've just met that you're about to share more than just his bed?

Find out in:

The Venetian One-Night Baby by Melanie Milburne

Heiress's Pregnancy Scandal by Julia James

Innocent's Nine-Month Scandal by Dani Collins

The Italian's Twin Consequences by Caitlin Crews

Greek's Baby of Redemption by Kate Hewitt

His Two Royal Secrets by Caitlin Crews

Look for more One Night With Consequences stories coming soon!

Sharon Kendrick

THE ARGENTINIAN'S BABY OF SCANDAL

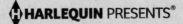

Recycling programs
for this product may
not exist in your area.

ISBN-13: 978-1-335-53851-2

The Argentinian's Baby of Scandal

First North American publication 2019

Printed in U.S.A.

www.Harlequin.com

Sharon Kendrick once won a national writing competition by describing her ideal date: being flown to an exotic island by a gorgeous and powerful man. Little did she realize that she'd just wandered into her dream job! Today she writes for Harlequin, and her books feature often stubborn but always *to-die-for* heroes and the women who bring them to their knees. She believes that the best books are those you never want to end. Just like life...

Books by Sharon Kendrick

Harlequin Presents

The Italian's Christmas Housekeeper

Conveniently Wed!

Bound to the Sicilian's Bed
The Greek's Bought Bride

One Night With Consequences

The Pregnant Kavakos Bride
The Italian's Christmas Secret
Crowned for the Sheikh's Baby

Secret Heirs of Billionaires

The Sheikh's Secret Baby

Wedlocked!

The Sheikh's Bought Wife

The Legendary Argentinian Billionaires

Bought Bride for the Argentinian

Visit the Author Profile page
at Harlequin.com for more titles.

This story is for Megan Crane, with whom I shared an unforgettable trip to the west of Ireland...and for Abby Green—the diva of Dublin!

CHAPTER ONE

LUCAS CONWAY SURVEYED the blonde who was standing in front of him and felt nothing, even though her eyes were red-rimmed and her cheeks wet with tears.

He felt a pulse beat at his temple.

Nothing at all.

'Who let you in?' he questioned coldly.

'Y-your housekeeper,' she said, her mouth working frantically as she tried to contain yet another sob. 'The one with the messy hair.'

'She had no right to let anyone in,' Lucas returned, briefly wondering how the actress could be so spiteful about someone who'd supposedly done her a good turn. But that was women for you—they never lived up to the promise of how they appeared on the outside. They were all teeth and smiles and then, when you looked beneath the surface, they were as shallow as a spill of water. 'I told her

I didn't want to be disturbed.' His voice was cool. 'Not by anyone. I'm sorry, Charlotte, but you'll have to leave. You should never have come here.'

He rose to his feet, because now he felt something, and it felt like the fury which had been simmering inside him for days. Although maybe fury was the wrong word to use. It didn't accurately describe the hot clench to his heart when he'd received the letter last week, did it? Nor the unaccustomed feeling of dread which had washed over him as he'd stared down at it. Memories of the past had swum into his mind. He remembered violence and discord. Things he didn't want to remember. Things he'd schooled himself to forget. But sometimes you were powerless when the past came looking for you...

His mouth was tight as he moved out from behind his desk, easily dwarfing the fair-haired beauty who was staring up at him with beseeching eyes. 'Come with me. I'll see you out.'

'Lucas—'

'Please, Charlotte,' he said, trying to inject his voice with the requisite amount of compassion he suspected was called for but failing—for he had no idea how to replicate this kind of emotion. Hadn't he often been accused of being unable to show *any* kind of feeling for another person—unless you counted desire, which was only ever temporary? He held back his sigh. 'Don't make this any more difficult than it already is.'

Briefly, she closed her swollen eyelids and nodded and he could smell her expensive perfume as he ushered her out of his huge office, which overlooked the choppy waters of Dublin Bay. And when she'd followed him—sniffling—to the front door, she tried one last time.

'Lucas.' Her voice trembled. 'I have to tell you this because it's important and you need to know it. I know there isn't anyone else on the scene and I've missed you. Missed being with you. What we had was good and I… I love you—'

'No,' he answered fiercely, cutting her short before she could humiliate herself any further. 'You don't. You can't. You don't really know me and if you did, you certainly wouldn't love me. I'm sorry. I'm not the man for you. So do yourself a favour, Charlotte, and go and find someone who is. Someone who has the capacity to care for you in the way you deserve to be cared for.'

She opened her mouth as if to make one last appeal but maybe she read the futility of such a gesture in his eyes, because she nodded and began to stumble towards her sports car in her spindly and impractical heels. He stood at the door and watched her leave, a gesture which might have been interpreted as one of courtesy but in reality it was to ensure that she really did exit the premises in her zippy little silver car, which shattered the peace as it sped off in a cloud of gravel.

He glanced up at the heavy sky. The weather had been oppressive for days now and the dark and straining clouds were hinting at the storm to come. He wished it would. Maybe it would lighten the oppressive atmosphere, which was making his forehead slick with sweat and his clothes feel as if they were clinging to his body. He closed the door. And then he turned his attention to his growing vexation as he thought about his interfering housekeeper.

His temper mounting, Lucas went downstairs into the basement, to the kitchen—which several high-profile magazines were itching to feature in their lifestyle section—to find Tara Fitzpatrick whipping something furiously in a copper bowl. She looked up as he walked in and a lock of thick red hair fell into her eye, which she instantly blew away with a big upward gust of breath, without pausing in her whipping motion. Why the hell didn't she get it cut so that it didn't resemble a birds' nest? he wondered testily. And why did she insist on wearing that horrible housecoat while she worked? A baggy garment made from some cheap, man-made fibre, which he'd once told her looked like a relic from the nineteen fifties and completely swamped her slender frame.

'She's gone, then?' she questioned, her gaze fixed on his as he walked in.

'Yes, she's gone.' He could feel the flicker of irritation growing inside him again and, suddenly, Tara seemed the ideal candidate to take it out on. 'Why the hell did you let her in?'

She hesitated, the movement of her whisk stilling. 'Because she was crying.'

'Of course she was crying. She's a spoiled woman who is used to getting her own way and that's what women like her do when it doesn't happen.'

She opened her mouth as if she was about to say something and then appeared to change her mind, so that her next comment came out as a mild observation. 'You were the one who dated her, Lucas.'

'And it was over,' he said dangerously. 'Months ago.'

Again, that hesitation—as if she was trying her hardest to be diplomatic—and Lucas thought, not for the first time, what a fey creature she was with her amber eyes and pale skin and that mass of fiery hair. And her slender body, which always looked as if it could do with a decent meal.

'Perhaps you didn't make it plain enough that it was over,' she suggested cautiously, resting her whisk on the side of the bowl and shaking her wrist, as if it was aching.

'I couldn't have been more plain,' he said. 'I told her in person, in as kind a way as possible, and said that perhaps one day we could be friends.'

Tara made a clicking noise with her lips and shook her head. 'That was your big mistake.'

'My big mistake?' he echoed dangerously.

'Sure. Give a woman hope and she'll cling to it like a chimp swinging from tree to tree. Maybe if you weren't so devastatingly attractive,' she added cheerfully, resuming her beating with a ferocity which sent the egg whites slapping against the sides of the bowl, 'then your exes wouldn't keep popping up around the place like lost puppy dogs.'

He heard the implicit criticism in his house-keeper's voice and the tension which had been mounting inside him all week now snapped. 'And maybe if you knew your place, instead of acting like the mistress of my damned house, then you wouldn't have let her in in the first place,' he flared as he stormed across the kitchen to make himself a cup of coffee.

Know her place?

Tara stopped beating as her boss's icy note of censure was replaced by the sound of grinding coffee beans and a lump rose in her throat, because he'd never spoken to her that way before—not in all the time she'd worked for him. Not with that air of impatient condemnation as if she were some trouble-some minion who was more trouble than she was worth. As she returned his gaze she swal-lowed with confusion and, yes, with hurt—and how stupid was that? Had she thought she was safe from his legendary coldness and a tongue which could slice out sharp words like a knife cutting through a courgette? Well, yes. She had. She'd naively imagined that, because she served him meals and ironed his shirts and made sure that his garden was carefully weeded and bright with flowers, he would never treat her with the disdain he seemed to direct at most women. That she had a special kind of place in his heart—when it was clear that Lucas Conway had no heart at all. And wasn't the fact of the matter that he'd been in a foul mood for this past week and growing snappier by the day? Ever since that official-looking letter had arrived from the United States and he'd disappeared into his office for a long time, before emerging with a haunted look darkening the spectacular verdant gleam of his eyes?

She ran a wooden spoon around the side of the bowl and then gave the mixture another half-hearted beat. She told herself she shouldn't let his arrogance or bad mood bother her. Maybe that was how you should expect a man to behave when he was as rich as Lucas Conway—as well as being the hottest lover in all of Ireland, if you were to believe the things people whispered about him.

Yet nobody really knew very much about the Dublin-based billionaire, no matter how hard they tried to find out. Even the Internet provided little joy—and Tara knew this for a fact because she'd looked him up herself on her ancient laptop, soon after she'd started working for him. His accent was difficult to figure out, that was for sure. He definitely wasn't Irish, and there was a faint hint of transatlantic drawl underpinning his sexy voice. He spoke many languages—French, Italian and Spanish as well as English—though, unlike Tara, he knew no Gaelic. He was rumoured to have been a bellhop, working in some fancy Swiss hotel, in the days before he'd arrived in Ireland to make his fortune but Tara had never quite been able to believe this particular rumour. As if someone like Lucas Conway would ever work as a bellhop! He was also reputed to have South American parentage—and with his tousled dark hair and the unusual green eyes which contrasted so vividly with his glowing olive skin, that was one rumour which would seem to be founded in truth.

She studied him as the machine dispensed a cup of his favoured industrial-strength brew of coffee. He'd had more girlfriends than most men had socks lined up in a top drawer of their bedroom, and was known for his exceptionally low boredom threshold. Which might explain why he'd dumped the seemingly perfect Charlotte when she—like so many others before her—had refused to get the message that he had no desire to be married. Yet that hadn't stopped her sending him a Valentine's card, had it—or arranging for a case of vintage champagne to be delivered on his birthday? 'I don't even particularly *like* champagne,' had been his moody aside to Tara as he'd peered into the wooden case, and she remembered thinking how ungrateful he could be.

Yet it wasn't just women of the sexy and supermodel variety who couldn't seem to get enough of him. Men liked him, too—and old ladies practically swooned whenever he came into their vicinity. Yet through all the attention he received, Lucas Conway always remained slightly aloof to the adulation which swirled around him. As if he was observing the world with the objectivity of a scientist, and, although nobody would ever have described him as untouchable, he was certainly what you might call unknowable.

But up until now he'd always treated her with respect. As if she mattered. Not as if she were just some skivvy working in his kitchen, with no more than two brain cells to rub together. The lump in her throat got bigger. Someone who didn't *know her place*.

Was that how he really saw her?

How others saw her?

She licked lips which had suddenly grown dry. Was that how she saw herself? The misfit from the country. The child who had grown up with the dark cloud of shame hanging over her. Who'd been terrified people were going to find her out, which was why she had fled to the city just as soon as she was able.

She told herself to leave it. To just nod politely and Lucas would vacate the kitchen and it would all be forgotten by the time she produced the feather-light cheese soufflé she was planning to serve for his dinner, because he wasn't going out tonight. But for some reason she couldn't leave it. Something was nagging away at her and she didn't know what it was. Was it the strange atmosphere which had descended on the house ever since that letter had arrived for him, and she'd heard the sound of muffled swearing coming from his office? Or was it something to do with this weird weather they'd been having, which was making the air seem as heavy as lead? Her heart missed a beat, because maybe it was a lot more basic than that. Maybe it all stemmed from having seen someone from home walking down Grafton Street yesterday, when she'd been window-shopping on her afternoon off.

Tara had nearly jumped out of her skin when she'd spotted her—and she was easy to spot. At school, Mona O'Sullivan had always been destined for great things and her high-heeled shoes and leather trench coat had borne out her teacher's gushing prophesy as she'd sashayed down Dublin's main street looking as if she didn't have a care in the world. A diamond ring had glittered like a giant trophy on her engagement finger and her hair had been perfectly coiffed.

Tara had ducked into a shop doorway, terrified Mona would see her and stop, before asking those probing questions which always used to make her blush to the roots of her hair and wish the ground would open up and swallow her. Questions which reminded Tara why she was so ashamed of the past she'd tried so desperately to forget. But you could never forget the past, not really. It haunted you like a spectre—always ready to jump out at you when you were least expecting it. It waited for you in the sometimes sleepless hours of the night and it lurked behind the supposedly innocent questions people put to you, which were anything but innocent. Was that why she had settled for this safe, well-paid job tucked away on the affluent edge of the city, where nobody knew her?

She wondered if her gratitude for having found such a cushy job had blinded her to the fact that she was now working for a man who seemed to think he had the right to talk to her as if she were nothing, just because he was in a filthy mood.

She stilled her spoon and crashed the copper bowl down on the table, aware that already the air would be leaving those carefully beaten egg whites—but suddenly she didn't care. Perhaps she'd been in danger of caring a bit too much what Lucas Conway had for his supper, instead of looking after herself. 'Then maybe you should find yourself someone who does know their place,' she declared.

Lucas turned round from the coffee machine with a slightly bemused look on his face. 'I'm sorry?'

She shook her head. 'It's too late for an apology, Lucas.'

'I wasn't apologising,' he ground out. 'I was trying to work out what the hell you're talking about.'

Now he was making her sound as if she were incapable of stringing a coherent sentence together! 'I'm talking about *knowing my place,*' Tara repeated, with an indignation which felt new and peculiar but oddly... *liberating.* 'I was trying to be kind to Charlotte because she was crying, and because I've actually spent several months of my life trying to wash her lipstick out of your pillowcases—so it wasn't like she was a complete stranger to me. And I once found one of her diamond studs when it was wedged into the floorboards of the dining room and she bought me a nice big bunch of flowers as a thank-you present. So what was I expected to do when she turned up today with mascara running all down her cheeks?' She glared at him. 'Turn her away?'

'Tara—'

'Do you think she was in any fit state to drive in that condition—with her eyes full of tears and her shoulders heaving?'

'Tara. I seem to have missed something along the way.' Lucas put his untouched coffee cup down on the table with as close an expression to incomprehension as she'd ever seen on those ruggedly handsome features. 'What's got into you all of a sudden?'

Tara still didn't know. Was it something to do with the dismissive way her boss's gaze had flicked over her admittedly disobedient hair when he'd walked into the kitchen? As if she were not a woman at all, but some odd-looking robot designed to cook and clean for him. She wondered if he would have looked like that if Mona O'Sullivan had been standing there whipping him up a cheese soufflé, with her high heels and her luscious curves accentuated by a tight belt.

But you dress like a frump deliberately, a small voice in her head reminded her. *You always have done. You were taught that the safest way to be around men was to make yourself look invisible and you heeded that lesson well. So what do you expect?*

And suddenly she saw exactly what she might expect. More of the same for the countless days which lay ahead of her. More of working her fingers to the bone for a man who didn't really appreciate her—and that maybe it was time to break out and reach for something new. To find herself a job in a big, noisy house with lots of children running around—wouldn't that be something which might fulfil her?

'I've decided I need a change of direction,' she said firmly.

'What are you talking about?'

Tara hesitated. Lucas Conway might be the biggest pain in the world at times, but surely he would give her a glowing reference as she'd worked for him since she'd been eighteen years old—when she'd arrived in the big city, slightly daunted by all the traffic, and the noise. 'A new job,' she elaborated.

He narrowed his stunning eyes—eyes as green as the valleys of Connemara. 'A new job?'

'That's right,' she agreed, thinking how satisfying it was to see the normally unflappable billionaire looking so perplexed. 'I've worked for you for almost six years, Lucas,' she informed him coolly. 'Surely you don't expect me to still be cooking and cleaning for you when you reach retirement age?'

From the deepening of his frown, he was clearly having difficulty getting his head around the idea of retirement and, indeed, Tara herself couldn't really imagine this very vital man ever stopping work for long enough to wind down.

'I shouldn't have spoken to you so rudely,' he said slowly. 'And that *is* an apology.'

'No, you shouldn't,' she agreed. 'But maybe you've done me a favour. It's about time I started looking for a new job.'

He shook his head and gave a bland but determined smile. 'You can't do that.'

Tara stilled. It was a long time since anyone had said those words to her, but it was the refrain which had defined her childhood.

You can't do that, Tara.

You mustn't do that, Tara.

She had been the scapegoat—carrying the can for the sins of her mother and of her grandmother before her. She had been expected to nod and keep her head down, never to make waves. To be obedient and hardworking and do as she was told. To stay away from boys because they only brought trouble with them.

And she'd learned her lessons well. She'd never been in a relationship. There hadn't been anyone to speak of since she'd arrived in Dublin and had gone on a few disastrous dates, encouraged by her friend Stella. She tried her best to forget the couple of encounters she'd shared with one of the farm hands back home, just before she'd left for the big city and landed the first job she'd been interviewed for. The agency had warned her that Lucas Conway was notoriously difficult to work for and she probably wouldn't last longer than the month but somehow she had proved them wrong. She earned more money than she'd ever imagined just by keeping his house clean, his shirts ironed and by putting a hot meal in front of him, when he wasn't gallivanting around the globe. It wasn't exactly brain surgery, was it?

On that first morning she had slipped on her polyester housecoat and, apart from a foreign holiday every year, that was where she'd been ever since, in his beautiful home in Dalkey. She frowned. Why did Lucas even *own* a place this big when he lived in it all on his own, save for her, carefully hidden away at the top of the vast house like someone in a Gothic novel? It wasn't as if he were showing any signs of settling down, was it? Why, she'd even seen him recoil in horror when his friend Finn Delaney had turned up one day with his wife Catherine and their brand-new baby.

'You can't stop me from leaving, Lucas,' she said, with a touch of defiance. 'I'll work my month's notice and you can find someone else. That won't be a problem—people will be queuing up around the block for a job like this. You know they will.'

Lucas looked at her and told himself to just let her go, because she was right. There had been dozens of applicants for the job last time he'd advertised and nothing much had changed in the years since Tara had been working for him, except that his bank balance had become even more inflated and he could easily afford to hire a whole battalion of staff, should the need arise.

But the young redhead from the country did more than just act as his housekeeper—sometimes it felt as if she kept his whole life ticking over. She didn't mind hard work and once he had asked her why she sometimes got down on her hands and knees to scrub the kitchen floor, when there was a perfectly serviceable mop to be had.

'Because a mop won't reach in the nooks and crannies,' she'd answered, looking at him as if he should have known something as basic as that.

He frowned. She wasn't just good at her job, she was also reliable, and no laundry could ever press a shirt as well as Tara Fitzpatrick did. It was true that sometimes she chattered too much—but on the plus side, she didn't go out as often as other young women her age so she was always available when he needed her. If he asked her to cook when he had people over for dinner she happily obliged—and her culinary repertoire had greatly improved since he'd arranged for her to go on an upmarket cookery course, after pointing out there were other things you could eat, rather than meat pie. As far as he knew, she never gossiped about him and that was like gold to him.

He didn't want her to leave.

Especially not now.

He felt the pound of his heart.

Not when he needed to go to the States to deal with the past, having been contacted by a lawyer hinting at something unusual, which had inexplicably filled him with dread. A trip he knew couldn't be avoided, no matter how much he would have preferred to. But the attorney's letter had been insistent. He swallowed. He hadn't been back to New York for years and that had been a deliberate choice. It was too full of memories. Bitter memories. And why confront stuff which made you feel uncomfortable, when avoidance was relatively simple?

Lucas allowed his gaze to skim down over the old-fashioned denim jeans Tara wore beneath her housecoat. Baggy and slightly too short, they looked as if they'd be more appropriate for working on a farm. No wonder she'd never brought a man back in all the time she worked for him when injecting a little glamour into her appearance seemed to be an unknown concept to her. And wasn't that another reason why he regarded her as the personification of rock-like reliability? She wasn't surreptitiously texting when she should have been working, was she? Nor gazing into space vacantly, mooning over some heartbreaker who'd recently let her down. Despite her slender build, she was strong and fit and he couldn't contemplate the thought of trying to find a replacement for her, not when he was focussed on that damned letter.

He wondered how much money it would take to get her to change her mind, and then frowned. Because in that way Tara seemed different from every other woman he'd ever had dealings with. She didn't openly lust after expensive clothes or belongings—not if her appearance was anything to go by. She wore no jewellery at all and, as far as he knew, she must be saving most of the salary he paid her, since he'd seen no signs of conspicuous spending—unless you counted the second-hand bicycle she'd purchased within a fortnight of coming to live here. The one with the very loud and irritating bell.

Lucas wasn't particularly interested in human nature but that didn't mean he couldn't recognise certain aspects of it, and it seemed to him that a woman who wasn't particularly interested in money would be unlikely to allow a salary increase to change her mind.

And then he had an idea. An idea so audacious and yet so brilliant that he couldn't believe it hadn't occurred to him before. Sensing triumph, he felt the flicker of a smile curving the edges of his mouth.

'Before you decide definitely to leave, Tara,' he said, 'why don't we discuss a couple of alternative plans for your future?'

'What are you talking about?' she questioned suspiciously. 'What sort of plans?'

His smile was slow and, deliberately, he made it reach his eyes. It was the smile he used when he was determined to get something and it was rare enough to stop people in their tracks. Women sometimes called it his killer smile. 'Not here and not now—not when you're working,' he said—a wave of his hand indicating the rows of copper pans which she kept so carefully gleaming. 'Why don't we have dinner together tonight so we can talk about it in comfort?'

'Dinner?' she echoed, with the same kind

of horrified uncertainty she might have used if he'd suggested they both dance naked in Phoenix Park. 'You're saying you want to have dinner with me?'

It wasn't exactly the way he would have expressed it—but want and need were pretty interchangeable, weren't they? Especially to a man like him. 'Why not?' he questioned softly. 'You have to eat and so do I.'

Her gaze fell to the collapsing mixture in her bowl. 'But I'm supposed to be making a cheese soufflé.'

'Forget the soufflé,' he gritted out. 'We'll go to a restaurant. Your choice,' he added magnanimously, for he doubted she would ever have set foot inside one of Dublin's finer establishments. 'Why don't you book somewhere for, say, seven-thirty?'

She was still blinking at him with disbelief, her pale lashes shuttering those strange amber eyes, until at last she nodded with a reluctance which somehow managed to be mildly insulting. Since when did someone take so long to deliberate about having dinner with him?

'Okay,' she said cautiously, with the air of someone feeling her way around in the dark. 'I don't see why not.'

CHAPTER TWO

THE AIR DOWN by the River Liffey offered no cooling respite against the muggy oppression of the evening and Lucas scowled as they walked along the quayside, unable to quite believe where he was. When he'd told Tara to choose a restaurant, he'd imagined she would immediately plump for one of Dublin's many fine eating establishments. He'd envisaged drawing up outside a discreetly lit building in one of the city's fancier streets with doormen springing to attention, instead of heading towards a distinctly edgy building which stood beside the dark gleam of the water.

'What is this place?' he demanded as at last they stopped beneath a red and white sign and she lifted her hand to open the door.

'It's a restaurant. A Polish restaurant,' she supplied, adding defensively, 'You told me to choose somewhere and so I did.'

He wanted to ask why but by then she had pushed the door open and a tinny bell was announcing their arrival. The place was surprisingly full of mainly young diners and an apple-cheeked woman in a white apron squealed her excitement before approaching and flinging her arms around Tara as if she were her long-lost daughter. A couple of interminable minutes followed, during which Lucas heard Tara hiss, *'My boss...'* which was when the man behind the bar stopped pouring some frothy golden beer to pierce him with a suspicious look which was almost challenging.

Lucas felt like going straight back out the way he had come in but he was hungry and they were being shown to a table which was like a throwback to the last century—with its red and white checked tablecloth and a dripping candle jammed into the neck of an empty wine bottle. He waited until they were seated before he leaned across the table, his voice low.

'Would you mind telling me why you chose to come and eat here out of all places in Dublin?' he bit out.

'Because Maria and her husband were very kind to me when I first came to the city and didn't know many people. And I happen to like it here—there's life and bustle and colour on the banks of the river. Plus it's cheap.'

'But I'm paying, Tara,' he objected softly. 'And budget isn't an option. You know that.'

Tara pursed her lips and didn't pass comment even though she wanted to suggest that maybe budget *should* be an option. That it might do the crazily rich Lucas Conway good to have to eat in restaurants which didn't involve remortgaging your house in order to pay the bill—that was if you were lucky enough to actually *have* a mortgage, which, naturally, she didn't. She felt like telling him she'd been terrified of choosing the kind of place she knew he usually frequented because she simply didn't have the kind of wardrobe—or the confidence—which would have fitted into such an upmarket venue. But instead she just pursed her lips together and smiled as she hung her handbag over the back of her chair, still pinching herself to think she was here.

With him.

Her boss.

Her boss who had turned the head of everyone in the restaurant the moment he'd walked in, with his striking good looks and a powerful aura which spoke of wealth and privilege.

She shook her hair, which she'd left loose, and realised that for once he was staring at her as if she were a real person, rather than just part of the fixtures and fittings. And how ironic it should be that this state of affairs had only come about because she'd told him she was leaving, which had led to him bizarrely inviting her to dinner. Did he find it as strange as she did for them to be together in a restaurant like this? she wondered. Just as she wondered if he would be as shocked as she was to discover that, for once. she was far from immune to his physical appeal.

So why was that? Why—after nearly six years of working for him when her most common reaction towards him had been one of exasperation—should she suddenly start displaying all the signs of being attracted to him? Because she prided herself on not being like all those other women who stared at him lustfully whenever he swam into view. It might have had something to do with the fact that he had very few secrets from her. She did his laundry. She even ironed his underpants and she'd always done it with an unfeigned impartiality. At home it had been easy to stick him in the categories marked 'boss' and 'off-limits', because arrogant billionaires were way above her pay grade, but tonight he seemed like neither of these things. He seemed deliciously and dangerously accessible. Was it because they were sitting facing each other across a small table, which meant she was noticing things about him which didn't normally register on her radar?

Like his body, for example. Had she ever properly registered just how broad his shoulders were? She didn't think so. Just as the sight of two buttons undone on his denim shirt didn't normally have the power to bring her out in a rash of goosebumps. She swallowed. In the candlelight, his olive skin was glowing like dark gold and casting entrancing shadows over his high cheekbones and ruggedly handsome face. She could feel her throat growing dry and her breasts tightening and wondered what had possessed her to agree to have dinner with him tonight, almost as if the two of them were on a date.

Because he had been determined to have a meal with her and he was a difficult man to shift once he'd set his mind on something.

She guessed his agenda would be to offer her a big salary increase in an attempt to get her to stay. He probably thought she'd spoken rashly when she'd told him she was leaving, which to some extent was true. But while she'd been getting ready—in a recently purchased and discounted dress, which was a lovely pale blue colour, even if it was a bit big on the bust—she'd decided she wasn't going to let him change her mind. And that his patronising attitude towards her had been the jolt she needed to shake her out of her comfort zone. She needed to leave Lucas Conway's employment and do something different with her life. To get out of the rut in which she found herself, even though it was a very comfortable rut. She couldn't keep letting the past define her—making her too scared to do anything else. Because otherwise wouldn't she run the risk of getting to the end of her days, only to realise she hadn't lived at all? That she'd just followed a predictable path of service and duty?

'What would you like to drink?' she questioned. 'They do a very good vodka here.'

'Vodka?' he echoed.

'Why not? It's a tradition. I only ever have one glass before dinner and then I switch to water. And it's not as if you're driving, is it?' Not with his driver sitting in a nearby parking lot in that vast and shiny limousine, waiting for the signal that the billionaire was ready to leave.

'Okay, Tara, you've sold it to me,' he answered tonelessly. 'Vodka it is.'

Two doll-sized glasses filled with clear liquor were placed on the tablecloth in front of them and Tara raised hers to his—watching the tiny vessel gleam in the candlelight before lifting it to her lips. *'Na zdrowie!'* she declared before tossing it back in one and Lucas gave a faint smile before drinking his own.

'What do you think?' she questioned, her eyes bright.

'I think one is quite enough,' he said. 'And since you seem to know so much about Polish customs, why don't you choose some food for us both?'

'Really?' she questioned.

'Really,' he agreed drily.

Lucas watched as she scrolled through the menu. She seemed to be enjoying showing off her knowledge and he recognised it was in his best interests to keep her mood elevated. He wanted her as compliant as possible and so he ate a livid-coloured beetroot soup, which was surprisingly good, and it wasn't until they were halfway through the main course that he put his fork down.

'Do you like it?' she questioned anxiously.

He gave a shrug. 'It's interesting. I've never eaten stuffed cabbage leaves before.'

'No, I suppose you wouldn't have done.' In the flickering light from the candle, her freckle-brushed face grew thoughtful. 'It's peasant food, really. And I suppose you've only ever had the best.'

The best? Lucas only just managed to bite back a bitter laugh as he stared into her amber eyes. It was funny the assumptions people made. He'd certainly tried most of the fanciest foods the world had to offer—white pearl caviar from the Caspian Sea and matsutake mushrooms from Japan. He'd eaten highly prized duck in one of Paris's most famous restaurants and been offered rare and costly moose cheese on one of his business trips to Sweden. Even at his expensive boarding school, the food had been good—he guessed when people were paying those kinds of fees, it didn't dare be anything but good. But the best meals he'd ever eaten had been homemade and cooked by Tara, he realised suddenly.

Which was why he was here, he reminded himself.

The only reason he was here.

So why were his thoughts full of other stuff? Dangerous stuff, which made him glad he'd only had a single vodka?

He stared at her. Unusually, she'd left her hair loose so that it flowed down over her narrow shoulders and the candlelight had transformed the wild curls into bright spirals of orange flame. Tonight she seemed to have a particularly fragile air of femininity about her, which he'd never noticed before. Was that something to do with the fact that for once she was wearing a dress, instead of her habitual jeans or leggings? Not a particularly flattering dress, it was true—but a dress all the same. Pale blue and very simple, it suited her naturally slim figure, though it could have done with being a little more fitted. But the scooped neck showed a faint golden dusting of freckles on her skin and drew his attention to the neatness of her small breasts and, inexplicably, he found himself wondering what kind of nipples she had. Tiny beads of sweat prickled on his brow and, not for the first time, he wished that the impending storm would break. Or that this damned restaurant would run to a little air conditioning. With an effort he dragged his attention back to the matter in hand, gulping down some water to ease the sudden dryness in his throat.

'The thing is,' he said slowly, putting his glass down and leaning back in his seat, 'that I don't want you to leave.'

'I appreciate that and it's very nice of you to say so, but—'

'No, wait.' He cut through her words with customary impatience. 'Before you start objecting, why don't you at least listen to what I'm offering you first?'

She trailed her fork through a small mound of rice on her plate so it created a narrow valley, before looking up at him, a frown creasing her brow. 'You can't just throw more money at the problem and hope that it'll go away.'

'So we have a problem, do we, Tara?'

'I shouldn't have said that. It's nothing to do with you, not really. It's me.' She hesitated. 'I need a change, that's all.'

'And a change is exactly what I'm offering you.'

Her amber eyes became shuttered with suspicion. 'What do you mean?'

He took another sip of water. 'What if I told you that I'm going to be leaving Dublin for a while, because I have to go to the States?'

'You mean on business?'

'Partly,' he answered obliquely. 'I'm thinking of investing in some property there. I need to spread my money around—at least, that's what my financial advisors are telling me.'

'This wouldn't have anything to do with that letter, would it?' she questioned curiously.

He grew still. 'What letter?'

'The one…' The words came out in a rush, as if she'd been waiting for a chance to say them. 'The one which arrived from America last week.'

Lucas wondered if she'd noticed his reaction at the time. If she'd seen the shock which had blindsided him. It suddenly occurred to him how much of his life she must have witnessed over the years—a silent observer of all the things which had happened to him. And wasn't that another reason for keeping her onside? Bringing another stranger into his home would involve getting to know a new person and having to learn to trust them and that was something to be avoided, because he didn't give his trust easily. His mouth hardened and his jaw firmed. And it wasn't going to happen. No way. Not when there was a much simpler solution.

'I'm planning a minimum six-month stay and I'm thinking of renting an apartment because the idea of spending that long living in a hotel isn't what you'd call appealing.' He slanted her his rare, slow smile. 'And that's where you come in, Tara.'

'Where?' she questioned blankly.

'I want you to come to New York with me.' He paused. 'Be my housekeeper there and I'll increase your salary—'

'You pay me very generously at the moment.'

He shook his head with a trace of impatience. Who in their right mind ever pointed out that kind of thing to their employer? 'The cost of living is higher there,' he said. 'And this will give you the opportunity to try living in a brand-new city. This could be a win-win situation for both of us, Tara.'

He thought she might show excitement and more than a little gratitude, not a look of sudden suspicion, which hooded her eyes. Inexplicably, he found his gaze drawn to the delicate bowed outline of her lips, which he'd never really noticed before. Well, of course he hadn't. He'd never been this close to her before, had he? Close enough to detect her faint scent, which was like no other perfume he'd ever encountered. Nor realised that her clear skin was porcelain-pale apart from those few freckles which dusted the upturn of her nose. He shook his head, perplexed by the observation and by the inexplicable rise of heat in his blood.

'New York,' she said slowly.

'You said you wanted a change. Well, what greater change from Dublin town than living in the buzzing metropolis of Manhattan? Didn't you go on a trip there last Christmas?'

She nodded.

'And didn't you have a good time?'

Once again, Tara nodded. She'd saved up and gone with her friend Stella, who was a nanny in nearby Dun Laoghaire, and they'd done the whole New York holiday thing together. A fun-packed snow and shopping trip, marred only by the fact that Tara had fallen over on the ice rink outside the Rockefeller building and grazed both her knees. 'We had a very good time.'

'So what's stopping you from saying yes?' he probed.

Tara nibbled on the inside of her lip, reminding herself that her plan had been to get *away* from Lucas—not to sign up for more of the same. She needed to remove herself from the influence of a powerful man who was selfishly pursuing his own interests. He certainly wasn't thinking about what was best for *her* at the moment, was he? Only what was best for him.

And yet.

She ran her fingertip over the frosted surface of her water glass. If she looked at it objectively couldn't this be the best of all possible outcomes? A trip to a glamorous city she was already familiar with, without all the uncertainty of having to fix herself up with a job? Wouldn't a spell in America provide the inspiration she needed to turn her life around and decide what she wanted to do next?

But still she held back from saying yes because something seemed to have changed between her and Lucas tonight. Something she couldn't quite put her finger on because she had no experience of this sort of thing. Was she imagining the tension which was stoking up between the two of them, like when you threw a handful of kindling on the fire? She certainly wasn't imagining the heart-racing feeling she was getting whenever she stared into his gorgeous green eyes—not to mention the fact that her body was behaving in a way which wasn't normal. At least, not normal for her. Her nipples were aching and there was a delicious syrupy feeling deep in the very core of her. She could feel a weird kind of restlessness she'd never experienced before, which was making her want to squirm uncomfortably on the wooden seat, and she was having to concentrate very hard not to keep wondering what it would be like to be kissed by him.

Was it because they were in the falsely intimate setting of a candlelit restaurant, making her wish she'd chosen somewhere brighter? Or because she'd stupidly decided to wear a dress and wash her hair—as if this were a real date or something? And now she was left feeling almost *vulnerable*—as if she'd lost the protective barrier which surrounded her when she was working at his house and cleaning up after him.

He was still studying her with an impatient question in his eyes, as if he wasn't used to being kept waiting. Come to think of it—he wasn't.

'Well?' he demanded.

'Can I have some time to think about it?' she said.

He looked surprised and Tara guessed that most women wouldn't have thought twice about accompanying their billionaire boss to a glamorous foreign city with the offer of a pay-rise.

'How long do you want?' he demanded.

Tara chewed on her lip. Should she ask her friend Stella's advice? She certainly didn't have anyone else to ask. She'd been so young when her mother died that she hardly remembered her and her grandmother had passed away just before she'd come to work for Lucas. 'A few days?' she suggested and gave a little shrug. 'Maybe you'll change *your* mind in the meantime?'

'If you continue to prevaricate like this, then maybe I will,' he retorted, not bothering to hide his displeasure. 'Let's just get the bill and go, shall we?'

'Okay.' She rose to her feet. 'But I need to use the washroom first.'

Still unable to believe she wasn't grabbing at his job offer with eager hands, Lucas watched as she walked through the restaurant, his gaze mesmerised by the curve of her calves, which led down to the slenderest ankles he'd ever seen. Suddenly he could understand why men living in the Victorian age had found them highly arousing.

He told himself to look away but somehow he couldn't. Somehow Tara Fitzpatrick's back view seemed to be the most beautiful thing he'd looked at in a long time, with those red curls spilling wildly over her shoulders. Her dress was slightly creased from where she'd been sitting but it was brushing against a bottom firmed by hard work and regular cycling—a realisation which was rewarded by an unwanted hardening at his groin. What the hell was happening to him? he wondered irritably. Was it simple physical frustration? Had Charlotte's unexpected appearance at his house this afternoon reminded him just how long it had been since he'd had sex? He remembered their split, when he'd grown bored with her and bored with bedding her. Because despite the actress's undeniable beauty and sexual experience, hadn't making love to her sometimes felt as if he were making love to a mannequin? *And there hadn't been anyone since, had there?* Not even a flicker of interest had stirred in his blood, despite the many come-ons which regularly came his way.

With an impatient shake of his head, he glanced at his cell-phone to see what the markets were doing, but for once his attention was stubbornly refusing to focus and when he looked up, Tara was back. She must have attempted to brush the fiery curls into some kind of submission, because they looked half-tamed. Her eyes were bright and her air of youthful vitality made his heart clench with something he didn't recognise. Was it cynicism? He shook his head, confused now and slightly resentful because he'd come out tonight thinking this was going to be a straightforward exercise and it was turning into anything but.

'The bill, Tara,' he said impatiently. 'Have you asked for it?'

'I've done more than that.' She gave a wide smile. 'I've paid it.'

'You've paid it?' he repeated slowly.

'It's very reasonably priced in here,' she said. 'And it's the least I can do, since we came here in your car.'

As he followed her out of the restaurant—after a farewell even more ecstatic than their greeting—Lucas found himself trying to remember the last time a woman had offered to pay for a meal. Not recently, that was for sure. Not since those days when he'd had nothing and heiresses had sniffed around him like dogs surrounding a piece of fresh meat. When he'd been forced to leave his fancy school because there had been no money—or so he'd been told. But pride had made him refuse to accept the charity of women who had been hungry for his virile body. He'd fed himself. Sometimes he'd eaten the food left lying around after a meal in the directors' dining room. And sometimes he just used to go without. Tara had been wrong when she'd suggested he'd never eaten peasant food, he thought, the harsh reminder of those days making his jaw clench as his car purred smoothly down the quayside towards them.

But when he joined her on the back seat the bitter memories were dissolved by a rush of something far more potent. Lucas felt a beat of promise and of heady desire. Flaring his nostrils, he inhaled her subtle scent, which was more like soap than perfume. Half turning his head, he saw the brightness of her hair and suddenly he wanted to tangle his fingers in it. One slender thigh was placed tantalisingly close to his—a gesture he suspected was completely lacking in provocation—yet right now it seemed the sexiest thing he'd ever encountered. He swallowed as desire beat through him like an insistent flame and if it had been anyone else he might have reached out and caressed her. Touched her leg until she was squirming with pleasure and widening her thighs and whispering for him to touch her some more.

But this was Tara and he couldn't do that because she worked for him. *She worked for him.* She made his bed and cooked his meals. Ironed his shirts and kept his garden bright. She was an employee he wanted to accompany him to America. She wasn't a prospective lover—not by any stretch of the imagination. He stared straight ahead, attempting to compose himself as the traffic lights turned red.

Her heart pounding and her shoulders tense, Tara told herself to stop feeling so nervous as the powerful car purred through the city streets because *none of this was a big deal.* She'd just had dinner with her boss— that was all—and he'd just offered her a job in America, which was a massive compliment, wasn't it? She'd never been in his chauffeur-driven car before either, and travelling home in such luxury should have been a real treat. Yet she was finding it difficult to appreciate the soft leather or incredibly smooth suspension as they travelled through Dublin. All she could think about was how *different* Lucas seemed tonight and how her reaction towards him seemed to have undergone a dangerous and fundamental shift. From being a demanding employer, he seemed to have morphed into a man she was having difficulty tearing her eyes away from. For the first time ever, she could understand why he inspired such a devoted following among women. Suddenly, she *got* why someone as beautiful as Charlotte would be prepared to humiliate herself in order to wheedle herself a way back into his life.

And I don't want to feel this way, she thought. *I want to go back to the way it was before, when I tolerated him more than idolised him and was often infuriated by him.*

The car pulled into the driveway of his Dalkey house but instead of being relieved that the journey was over, all Tara could feel was a peculiar sense of disappointment. Blindly, she reached for the door handle, her usually dextrous fingers flailing miserably as she failed to locate it in the semi-darkness.

'Here,' said Lucas, sounding suddenly amused as he leaned across her to click a button. 'Let me.'

Of course. The door slid noiselessly open because it was an electronic door and didn't actually have a handle! What a stupid country girl she must seem. But Tara's embarrassment at her lack of savvy was exacerbated by a heart-stopping awareness as Lucas's arm brushed against hers. She swallowed. He'd touched her. *He'd actually touched her.* He might not have meant to but his fingers had made contact and where they had it felt like fire flickering against her skin.

Scrambling out of the car into an atmosphere even stickier than earlier, she cast a longing look towards the heavy sky, wishing it would rain and shatter this strange tension which seemed to be building inside her, as well as in the atmosphere. She scrabbled around in her handbag to fish out her key but her fingers were trembling as she heard a footfall behind her and Lucas's shadow loomed over her as she inserted it tremblingly into the lock.

'You're shaking, Tara,' he observed as she opened the door and stepped into the house.

'It's a cold night,' she said automatically, even though that wasn't true. But he didn't correct her with a caustic comment as he might normally have done.

And the strange thing was that neither of them moved to put on the main light once the heavy front door had swung shut behind them, and the gloom of the vast hallway seemed to increase the sense of unreality which had been building between them all evening.

There was something in the air. Something indefinable. Tara felt acutely aware of just how close Lucas was. His eyes were dark and gleaming as he stared down at her and she held her breath as, for one heart-stopping moment, she thought he was going to kiss her. She felt as if he was going to pull her into his arms and crush his lips down on hers.

But he didn't.

Of course he didn't.

Had she taken complete leave of her senses? He simply clicked the switch so that they were flooded with a golden light, which felt like a torch being shone straight into her eyes, and the atmosphere shattered as dramatically as a bubble being burst. A hard smile was playing at the edges of his lips and he nodded, as if her reaction was very familiar to him.

'Goodnight, Tara,' he said in an odd kind of voice. And as he turned away from her, she could hear the distant rumble of thunder.

CHAPTER THREE

THE NEXT FEW days were an agony of indecision as Tara tried to make up her mind whether or not to accept Lucas's job offer. She tried drawing up a list of pros and cons—which came up firmly weighted in favour of an unexpected trip to America with her boss. Next she canvassed her friend Stella, who told her she'd be mad not to jump at the chance of joining Lucas in New York.

'Why wouldn't you go?' Stella demanded as she folded up one of the tiny smocked dresses belonging to the twin baby girls she nannied for. 'You *loved* New York when we went last Christmas. Apart from the ice-rink incident, of course,' she added hastily. 'And that man really should have been looking where he was going. It's a no-brainer as far as I can see, so why the hesitation?'

Tara didn't answer. She thought how lame

it would sound if she confessed that something felt different between her and Lucas and that something unspoken and sexual seemed to have flowered between them that night. Or would it simply seem deluded and possibly arrogant to imply that Dublin's sexiest billionaire might be interested in someone like her?

But something *had* changed. She wasn't imagining it. The new awkwardness between them. The shadowed look around his eyes when she'd brought in his breakfast the morning after that crazy dinner, which had made her wonder if his night had been as sleepless as hers. The flickering glance he'd given her when she'd put the coffee pot down with trembling fingers before he'd announced that he was flying to Berlin later that morning and would be back in a couple of days—and could she possibly give him her answer about accompanying him to America by then?

'Yes, of course,' she'd answered stiffly, wondering why she was dragging her feet so much when she knew what she *ought* to say. She practised saying it over and over in her head.

It's a very kind offer, Lucas—but I'm going to have to say no.

Why?

Because... Because I've fallen in lust with you.

How ridiculous would that sound, even if it weren't coming from someone who could measure her sexual experience on the little finger of one hand?

But it was easier to shelve the decision and even easier when he wasn't around So Tara just carried on working and when she wasn't working, she did the kind of things she always did when Lucas was away. She swam in his basement pool and began to tidy up the garden for winter. She made cupcakes for a local charity coffee morning and went to Phoenix Park with Stella and her young charges. She listened to Lucas's voicemail telling her he'd be late back on Thursday night and not to bother making dinner for him.

And still the wretched weather wouldn't break. It was so heavy and sticky that you felt you couldn't breathe properly. As if it was pressing against your throat like an invisible pair of hands. Sweat kept trickling down the back of her neck and despite piling her rampant curls on top of her head, nothing she did seemed to make her cool.

On Thursday evening she washed her hair

and went to bed, listening out for the sound of Lucas's chauffeur, who had gone to collect him from the airport. It wasn't even that late, but several days of accumulated sleeplessness demanded respite and Tara immediately fell into a deep sleep, from which she was woken by a sudden loud crack, followed by a booming bang. Sitting bolt upright in bed, she tried to orientate herself, before the monochrome firework display taking place outside her bedroom window began to make sense. Of course. It was the storm. The long-awaited storm which had been building for days. Thank heavens. At least now the atmosphere might get a bit lighter.

Another flash of lightning illuminated her bedroom so that it looked like an old-fashioned horror film and almost immediately a clap of thunder echoed through the big house. The storm must be right overhead, she thought, just as heavy rain began to teem down outside the window. It sounded loud and rhythmical and oddly soothing and Tara sank back down onto the pillows and lay there with her eyes wide open, when she heard another crash. But this time it didn't sound like thunder. Her body tensed. This time it sounded distinctly like the sound of breaking glass.

Quickly, she got out of bed, her heart pounding and her bare toes gripping the floorboards. What if it was a burglar? This was a big house in a wealthy area and didn't they say thieves always chose opportunistic moments to break in? What better time than amid the dramatic chaos of a wild thunderstorm?

Pulling on her dressing gown, she knotted the belt tightly around her waist and wondered if she should go and wake Lucas. Of course she should—if he was back. Yet she was dreading knocking on his bedroom door in a way she would never have done before she'd agreed to have dinner with him. Back then—in that unenlightened and innocent time before she'd started to fantasise about him—she wouldn't have been in an angsty state of excitement, wondering what she'd find. She knew he didn't wear pyjamas because she did his laundry for him. And that was the trouble. She knew so much about him and yet not nearly enough.

Quietly, she pushed open her bedroom door and crept along the corridor, her head buzzing. At least she'd made up her mind about how to deal with his job offer—because no way could she join Lucas in America now, not if she was harbouring stupid ideas about what it would be like to…to…

She cocked her head and listened. Was that the creak of a footstep on the stairwell she could hear, or just the normal sounds of the big house settling down for the night? It was difficult to tell above the sound of the drumming rain. Peering over the bannister, she could see light streaming from Lucas's room on the floor below and she crept downstairs towards it.

She had just reached his door when a figure appeared at the top of the stairs and Tara nearly jumped out of her skin when she realised that Lucas was standing there wearing nothing but a pair of faded denims, which he had clearly just slung on, because the top button was undone. And his chest was bare. Gloriously and deliciously bare—his washboard abs as beautifully defined as the powerful curves of his forearms. Tara felt the sudden flip of her heart and was furious with herself—because wasn't it shocking to be noticing something like that at a time like this? She was supposed to be investigating a night-time disturbance, not eying up her half-naked boss like some kind of man-hungry desperado.

'Lucas!' she breathed. 'It's you.'

'Of course it's me—who else did you think it would be? Father Christmas?' he snapped. 'And what the hell are you doing, creeping around the place like a damned wraith?'

She was still flustered by the sight of him wearing so few clothes, and her reply came blurting out, the words tumbling over themselves in their eagerness to be said. 'I… I heard a crash from downstairs and I thought it might be…' she shrugged '…a burglar!'

'And you thought the best way to deal with some potentially violent nutter was to confront him with nothing more effective than an indignant look in your eyes?' His gaze bored into her. 'Are you out of your mind, Tara?'

Tara licked her bone-dry lips. Yes, that was a pretty accurate description of the way she was feeling right now. But she could hardly tell him the reason why, could she? She could hardly explain that her fixation about him had been so great that it hadn't left room in her head for anything else, and certainly not common sense. 'So what was the crash?' she questioned. 'Did you find out?'

Lucas scowled, aware that his body was

hardening in a way which was *not* what he wanted to happen. And the reason for his suddenly urgent desire was the most perplexing thing of all. Tara was standing there in some passion-killer of a dressing gown, which looked as if it had been made from an old bedspread, and yet a powerful sexual hunger was pumping through his veins. It defied all logic, he thought—just as his behaviour had done in the few days since they'd been apart. He'd been busy in Berlin, buying fleets of electric cars and planning to lease them out to businesses at a highly profitable rate. He'd had several high-powered meetings with the German transport minister and had been taken to an entrancing *Schloss*, situated outside the capital, where busty blondes had served them foaming tankards of beer. Yet all the time there had been a constant soundtrack playing in his mind as if it was on some infernal loop and giving him no peace. It had begun with Tara and ended with Tara and had involved plenty of X-rated images of how her pale and freckled body might look if it were naked in his bed.

Why the hell was he thinking so graphically about a woman he'd never even given a second glance to before?

Somehow he managed to drag his thoughts back to the present, realising that she was regarding him with a question in her eyes, and somehow he managed to dredge up a memory of what she'd asked him. 'It was something breaking in the kitchen,' he informed her tightly. 'You'd left a window in the pantry open and the wind made some figurine fall.'

'Oh, dear.' She bit her lip. 'I'd better go and tidy it up.'

'No. Leave it until morning,' he said firmly. 'You shouldn't be clearing up broken china at this time of night—though the ornament is beyond repair, I'm afraid.'

Tara nodded, her mouth working with an unexpected flare of emotion, despite all her mixed feelings about where that little statue had come from. She'd only put it there because she'd been planning to clean it tomorrow. 'Can't be helped.'

'Was it something special?'

It wasn't the kind of thing he usually asked and for a moment she almost told him about the figurine of St Christopher—the patron saint of travellers—which her mother had taken with her when she'd left for England, setting out on a life which was supposed to be so different from what she'd left behind. But why would you start explaining a woman's broken dreams to a man who probably wasn't really interested—and a man who was only half dressed? Wouldn't that lead to questions and then yet more questions, which might end up with her revealing telltale details about her background? And nobody wanted to hear those, least of all herself. She might as well write on a placard: *This is why I am such a freak.* She shook her head and turned away but not before the salty prickle of tears had stung her eyes.

Had Lucas seen it? Was that why his voice suddenly gentled in a way she'd never heard before?

'Tara?' he said.

Impatiently fisting away the tears, Tara didn't know what she'd been expecting but it wasn't for Lucas to turn her around to look at him. It was just a hand placed on her upper arm, through the thick barrier of her dressing gown. The type of reassuring gesture anyone might make to someone who was on the verge of crying, but it didn't feel remotely like that. It felt…*electric.* Tara had grown up in a house where physical contact was frowned upon, where nobody actually *touched* each other— and nobody had touched her in years. Was it that which made her response to Lucas so instant? Her blood was heating, like syrup on an open flame, and her body felt as if it were dissolving from the inside out. She sucked in a shuddered breath and somehow it seemed inevitable he should pull her into his arms. It was comfort, she told herself. That was all.

But it didn't feel like comfort. It felt like heaven. Like a taste of something she'd never quite believed in. He was so big and powerful—so warm and strong—that it seemed only natural to let her head fall to his shoulder and for her breath to fan the silken skin of his neck. Tara had no idea how long that wordless embrace lasted. It might have been a few seconds but, there again, it could have been longer. Suddenly he pushed her head away so he could look at her, his eyes searching her face long and hard, and she'd never seen him look so disorientated. As if he were in some weird kind of dream and was expecting to wake up at any minute.

But he didn't wake up—and neither did she. They remained standing in the same spot, staring into each other's eyes as if it were the first time they'd ever seen each other.

'You'd better go back to your own room,' he said unsteadily.

Afterwards, Tara would ask herself what had possessed her to behave in such an uncharacteristic way. Was it the certainty of knowing she wasn't going to be working for him much longer which made her throw caution to the wind? Or just the fact that she'd never felt like this before—as if her body were on fire with a burning need too powerful to be ignored? For once she wanted to cast aside the roles she'd been given in life. To forget the person she'd been taught to become. Obedient Tara. Wary Tara. The woman who had never stepped out of line because that way lay danger and she had been fearful of what might happen if she refused to comply.

But now there was no fear, only an audacity which felt newly minted and exhilarating.

'Why?' she questioned.

Her question hung in the air.

'You know why,' he ground out.

And somehow she did. Even though she had no experience of such matters, Tara could tell that Lucas Conway wanted her in exactly the same way as she wanted him. It was explicit in the tension which radiated from his powerful body and the hectic gleam which was glittering from his eyes. Her mouth was dry as she gazed at his lips and the temptation to kiss them was just too strong to resist. Because those lips held the tantalising promise of something else—something she was keen to explore. Suddenly she reached up to wind her arms around his neck, her thumbs stroking the dark waves of hair which covered the base of his neck, and she heard him suck in a breath.

'Go to bed, Tara,' he growled.

Again, that boldness. That strange, uncharacteristic boldness as she repeated her own guileless question. 'Why?'

'I don't want to take advantage of you.'

'We're not playing a game of tennis, Lucas.'

'You know what I mean,' he growled. 'I'm your employer.'

'Not right now you're not,' she declared fiercely. 'Unless you're planning on demanding I go and fix you a midnight snack or iron a shirt for you.'

An unexpected smile curved at his lips as Lucas realised how his humble housekeeper seemed determined to confound all his expectations tonight—in fact, to blow them clean away. She'd fearlessly come downstairs to tackle a potential thief like some kind of modern-day warrior queen. With her pale skin and red curls streaming down her back like a pre-Raphaelite painting, she looked fragile and ethereal and yet she was turning him on. Very, very much. And suddenly he couldn't stem his desire any longer, not with her slim body so near and her mouth so tantalisingly close. He angled his head to kiss her, wondering if he was breaking some kind of fundamental rule. Some unspoken moral code. And then he cursed himself for even posing such a stupid question. Of course he was. Big time. He knew that. But knowing didn't change anything—how could it when she was kissing him back with a hunger which felt as fierce as anything he'd ever encountered?

Her lips were as soft as petals and he could sense all the sweet promise in her slim young body. Already he felt as if he wanted to explode. As if he could tear that ugly dressing gown from her body and do it to her right there, up against the wall outside his bedroom. Yet something held him back and not just because this was the first time and instinct told him to savour it, in case there wasn't a repeat. There was also part of him—a growingly distant part of him, admittedly—which wondered if one of them was going to suddenly come to their senses. As if something would suddenly shatter this strange spell and leave them facing each other with an air of disbelief and embarrassment.

But that wasn't happening. The only thing on the agenda right now was that the kiss was growing deeper—and the first tentative thrust of her tongue was making his groin grow deliciously hard. Hell. What kind of sorcery was she wielding when she was doing so little? And why was her body still hidden from his hungry gaze, beneath the folds of that unspeakable dressing gown?

Pulling his mouth away from hers, he saw nothing but dazed compliance in her eyes and was unprepared for the ecstatic thundering of his heart in response. When was the last time he'd felt this…*excited* about having sex with a woman? Was it because this was the last thing he'd ever imagined happening, or because she was so different from anyone he'd ever been intimate with?

He thought about leading her to his bedroom in a way he'd done with other women countless times over the years, when instead he did something which had never happened before. Picking her up, he planted his foot in the centre of the door and kicked it wide open.

'Lucas!' breathed Tara, her voice sounding

almost shocked as he carried her towards his bed, which was softly illuminated by the glow of a nearby lamp.

'What's the matter, Tara?' he growled. 'Don't you like the masterful approach?'

She shook her head so that her curls shimmered down her back like a halo of fire and he could see her licking her lips before her next words came out with a rush of bravado. 'I don't like you kicking the paintwork when I'm the one who has to clean it!'

He laughed—which was extraordinary because he didn't usually associate humour with sex—but his mirth was quickly forgotten as he lowered her to her feet. Pulling open the sash of her dressing gown, he narrowed his eyes on discovering she wasn't naked underneath. Far from it. A baggy T-shirt of indeterminate colour hung to the middle of her lithe thighs. 'You certainly aren't dressed for seduction,' he observed wryly as he peeled it over her head.

'I'm right…right out of silk negligees,' she breathed as he smoothed his hands down over her ruffled curls.

Once again, he could hear a trace of vulnerability behind her flippant response and so he kissed her some more while he dealt with his zip, which was straining almost painfully over his hardness. He waited for her to offer to help him, but she didn't—and maybe that was a good thing. He wasn't sure he trusted anyone to touch him when he was this close to coming.

Kicking off his jeans, he urgently peeled back the duvet, sinking her down onto the mattress and wrapping his arms tightly around her so that they were skin-on-skin. He could hear her gasp as his erection sprang against her belly and for one last time he heard a whisper of warning in the recesses of his mind. *Are you sure you're doing the right thing?* But her long legs were tangling with his with unashamed excitement and when he slid his hand between her thighs, she was so wet and warm and slippery. He wasn't sure at all, he realised, but the only power on earth which could stop him now was Tara herself and, judging by the way she was writhing beneath him, that wasn't going to happen any time soon.

'Oh,' he said, his voice dipping with approval as he whispered his fingertip over the engorged little bud which was slick with desire.

'Oh,' echoed Tara as a shimmer of incredible sensation swept over her. Was this what had been spoken about with such venom when she'd been growing up? The most wicked thing in the world which could bring with it terrible consequences?

He lowered his lips to hers again and the sweetness of his kiss made her heart want to burst from her chest. How was it possible to *feel* this good? She closed her eyes in ecstasy as he began to kiss her breasts, his tongue flicking against one nipple so that it peaked into his mouth as if it had been made for just that purpose. She quivered as his fingertips skated over her skin, leaving a trail of goosebumps in their wake as he explored her breasts and belly and the jutting bones of her hips. Suddenly she wanted to touch him back in the same intimate way but she was shy and scared—wondering if her inexperience would put him off and bring this all to an abrupt end.

She thought: *Am I going to be passive about this, or am I going to be a participant?* For the first time in her life, couldn't she just go with what she wanted to do rather than thinking about what was the *right* thing to do? Fired by a fierce tide of hunger, she whispered her hand down his spine and then drifted her fingertips to the flat planes of his stomach. Did he sense she was going to move her hand further down to explore his hardness for the first time? Was that why he gave a low laugh of expectation?

In the soft light she could see the pale pole of his hardness contrasted vividly against the burnished hue of his olive skin and Tara wondered why she wasn't feeling the fear she had expected on seeing an aroused man for the first time in her life. Because this felt perfectly natural, that was why. This was what was *supposed* to happen between a man and a woman.

Tentatively, and with the lightness of touch which made her such a good pastry-maker, she started to stroke him—but he endured the exploratory skate of her fingers for no more than a minute before shaking his head.

'If you carry on doing that, this will not end well,' he growled softly, reaching out for a foil packet on the locker and tearing it open with impatient fingers. Then he lifted her up to position her over him, so she was intimately straddling him, his tip nudging against her new-found wetness.

Tara gasped as he splayed his hands over her breasts, his thumbs playing with her thrusting nipples, which instantly made her want to squirm with pleasure—although she wasn't exactly in the ideal position to do any squirming.

'Ride me, Tara,' he urged huskily. 'Ride me.'

She didn't get a chance to tell him she didn't really know what he was talking about because, suddenly, he was pulling her down onto him so that his erection was pushing deep inside her, as if he was done with talking and couldn't wait a second longer. Pushing up right into her so that he filled her completely, and the warm rush of unexpected pleasure was slightly offset by the unexpected shock of what was happening to her body. She could feel her muscles tense and the briefest split of pain. She closed her eyes and when she opened them again, she found Lucas staring up at her with an expression of disbelief on his rugged features and something else.

Was it regret?

Or was it anger?

'You're a virgin?' he bit out.

Breathlessly, she nodded.

He said something she didn't understand— she thought it might be in Italian, though what did she know?—and it sounded incredulous.

He put his hands on either side of her hips and for a moment she thought he was going to remove her from his body and tell her to get out. But he didn't. With a look of intense concentration on his face, he flipped her over onto her back while he was still inside her, displaying a skill which spoke volumes about his experience. And once she was on her back he smoothed away the wild disarray of curls from her face and stared down at her.

'I think I'd better be the one in charge from now on, don't you?' he said thickly.

She nodded, terrified of saying the wrong thing. Terrified he was going to stop. Because she couldn't bear that—not when those amazing feelings were building up inside her again and he was bending his head to kiss her more deeply than before. And she was floating now. Floating off into a sweet and strange new world where nothing existed except the sensation of Lucas Conway thrusting deep inside her, his mouth capturing hers in kiss after kiss. He moved slowly at first and then faster—as if her body was sending out an unspoken command which he correctly interpreted and acted upon.

She didn't think it would happen. Not the first time. She might have been innocent but she'd read all the magazine articles, like everyone else. And when it did, her orgasm was nothing like she'd expected. Because how could she ever have anticipated that something could feel this good? As if the sweet spasms which were racking her body had transformed her, so that for a moment she felt as if she'd redefined what it meant to be human.

Her fingers dug into the damp skin at his back and she kissed his neck over and over again as his own movements changed. His thrusts became more urgent and she heard his shuddered groan just before he collapsed on top of her. She wrapped her arms around him and in that moment she felt as if she'd tumbled into paradise and never wanted to leave. But nearly six years of a boss-employee relationship couldn't be dissolved in a couple of minutes and the unmistakable balance of power between them hadn't changed. So she lay there perfectly still and waited to hear what Lucas had to say.

CHAPTER FOUR

TARA STARED OUT at the sodden morning to where the previous night's storm had left the garden completely battered—as if some giant malevolent fist had pummelled the shrubs and flowers and left them leafless and sad. Gloomily surveying the damage to her previously well-tended shrubs, she found herself wondering if Lucas was in the air by now. If he was already beginning the process of forgetting her. Probably. No doubt it would be a speedy process in his case—less so in her own, she suspected—as she remembered the awkward words which had followed their passionate bout of sex.

It had been the worst conversation of her life—though of course she'd been too young to remember her grandmother telling her that her mammy was dead, which she supposed she must have done. Worse even than the time she'd discovered the truth about her tarnished legacy—not from the person who *should* have told her, but from a sniggering trio of bullies on a freezing cold school playground in the rural wilds of Ballykenna.

Nope. She sighed as she turned away from the window. It had been an all-time low to hear Lucas's chilly statement as he'd coolly detached himself from her satiated and naked body and rolled to the other side of the bed, his voice as distant as the great space which had suddenly appeared between them. And, just as she must have done twenty times over—she found herself reliving that post-sex scenario, word by excruciating word.

It had started with Lucas. A flat, hard assessment which had allowed no room for manoeuvre.

'That should never have happened.'

The trouble was that on one level she had agreed with him. It shouldn't. While on another level…

The flip side of the coin was that she'd been lying there, basking in emotion and reaction and a million other things besides. She'd felt fulfilled and relieved—yes, relieved—grateful that she was capable of feeling all the stuff other women felt and that her body was functioning just fine. For a few crazy, misplaced minutes before her boss had spoken, she'd actually been thinking that maybe she *could* go to New York with him, after all. That perhaps they could carry on doing...well, doing *this*. All right, it hadn't been the most conventional beginning in the world—but the world wasn't a conventional place these days and who was to say they couldn't have some kind of relationship, even if it didn't last? But Lucas hadn't wanted to hear that. He hadn't wanted to hear anything which smacked of eagerness. Presumably what he'd wanted was an unflappable response which echoed his own sentiments—one which reassured him that she wasn't about to start reading something into a foolish act of passion which meant nothing in the grand scheme of things.

'No,' she'd said slowly. 'I suppose it shouldn't.'

'I can't believe what we just did. I just can't believe it.' He had shaken his tousled dark head. 'I should have—'

'Honestly, Lucas, you don't have to explain,' she had butted in quickly, her voice sounding much sharper than usual and he'd turned his head to look at her in surprise, as if thinking she didn't usually talk that way to him, which of course she didn't. But then, they weren't usually lying buck-naked in bed, were they? And because she couldn't bear the thought of him voicing any more regrets and leaving her with nothing but uncomfortable memories of her first ever sexual experience—which happened to have completely blown her away—she had somehow forced a smile to her lips. She'd even managed a half-shrug, glad that her expression was mostly hidden by the thick fall of her curls. 'Things got out of hand, that's all. It's not a big deal. Really.'

'But you were a *virgin*, Tara.'

'So what? Everybody is a virgin at some point in their life. I had to lose it some day.'

'But not with…'

His words had tailed off but she'd wondered what he had been about to say. Not with someone like me, probably. Someone who was completely out of her league. A commitment-phobe billionaire who normally dated the kind of women most men lusted after, not a skinny redheaded employee who'd hardly even been kissed before.

'I can't offer you anything, Tara,' he had continued fiercely. 'If that's what you're thinking.'

How *dared* he presume to know what she was thinking? Hiding her hurt behind righteous indignation, Tara had decided to fight against the negative opinion he seemed to be forming of her.

'You thought I was holding out for the man I'd one day marry?' His look of surprise had told her she'd judged it correctly. 'That I wanted to trade my innocence for a big white dress and a triumphant march down the aisle? You think the only reason we country girls come to the city is because we're looking for a husband? Well, don't worry, Lucas. I'm not— and if I was, I wouldn't choose someone who clearly has no intention of ever settling down. Just like I'm not expecting anything to come of this. You're right—it shouldn't have happened and it certainly won't happen again. For one thing, you're off to New York, aren't you? And I'm staying here in Dublin to find myself another job, which was always the plan.'

Unlike that night over dinner, this time he hadn't attempted to persuade her to stay and Tara felt angry at herself for having supposed he might. And hurt, too. That was the stupid thing. Her heart gave a funny little twist. He obviously couldn't wait to put as many air miles between them as possible. She'd thought she couldn't possibly feel any worse than she did, and then he had proceeded to rub salt into the wound by being unusually considerate.

'Look, I don't want you to feel you have to rush into anything.' His words had been careful but he had seemed oblivious to the irony in them as he'd reached out to glance at his watch. 'You must use the house here in Dalkey for as long as it takes you to find a job you really like. I'll be away for at least six months and I don't want you feeling as if you've got to grab the first thing which comes to hand just to get away from here.'

He'd made her feel like a charity case but somehow Tara had hidden her humiliation behind a tight smile as she'd scrambled off the bed. 'Thanks, I appreciate it.'

'Tara?'

'What?' Her voice had been toneless as she'd turned around to answer his deep command. And wasn't it crazy how the human spirit continued to hope no matter how much the odds were stacked against it? Hadn't she secretly been praying he was going to tell her to get right back into bed when one look at the shuttered indifference on his face had told her that any such hope was pointless? 'What is it?' she'd said.

He had shrugged, even though she'd been able to see his body shift uncomfortably on the bed and the rigid outline of his erection beneath the sheet had been abundantly clear. She had felt herself blush and had been grateful that the dim light of the room had hidden her embarrassment.

'Nothing,' he'd growled. 'It doesn't matter.'

So she had picked up her abandoned dressing gown and T-shirt and returned to her room without another glance at the naked man on the rumpled bed, and if she'd thought he might come running after her—well, he hadn't done that either.

In the morning she'd overslept—which she *never* did—and when she'd gone downstairs, she'd found a note lying on the table. A simple note. A note which was damning despite its air of considered politeness. Or maybe because of it.

Tara,
In view of what happened last night, I've brought my trip to New York forward by a few days. I'm sure you'll understand the reasons why.

Good luck with all that you do—
you've been the best housekeeper I've
ever had and any references I provide
will reflect that opinion.

I've paid you in advance for six
months, so take your time choosing your
next position.
Lucas

What position was he talking about? she'd
wondered with a mild tinge of hysteria as
she'd crumpled the note in her palm before
hurling it into the fire where it had com-
busted into a bouquet of bright flames. The
one which involved her straddling him before
taking him deep inside her body?

But recriminations and casting blame were
going to get her nowhere. She needed to think
clearly and objectively and, most of all, she
needed a new job. She went to a couple of
employment agencies and scrolled through
the newspapers for domestic vacancies, but
nothing compared to working for Lucas. She
even went on a couple of interviews but her
heart wasn't in it and despite her glowing references she was turned down for both jobs,
which didn't exactly do wonders for her self-
esteem.

She was longing to confide in Stella but something held her back. Was it because she thought her friend might be shocked by what she'd done—essentially enjoyed a night of casual sex with her employer? Stella couldn't be more shocked than she was herself, Tara thought grimly as she polished the fine furniture in Lucas's sitting room, trying to keep herself busy. And she discovered very quickly that it was easy to procrastinate. To act as if nothing had really changed, except that it had.

Something had *really* changed.

Her periods had always been as regular as clockwork and so she was concerned from the very first day of being late. But there again, it was weird how your mind did its best to protect you by concealing the truth and cloaking it in all kinds of possibilities. She told herself that there'd been so much upheaval lately it was no wonder she was a little out of sorts. She blamed the sudden dip in the temperature as autumn suddenly swept through the city. She managed to keep these various myths alive for a whole fortnight. It was only when she'd been unable to keep her breakfast down, or her lunch for that matter—and Stella had popped round unexpectedly to find her sitting white-faced in the kitchen—that the whole horrible truth came tumbling out, though it still needed a little prompting.

'So. Are you going to tell me what's going on, Tara?' her friend demanded. 'About why you're looking so awful and acting so distracted?'

Licking her tongue over bone-dry lips, Tara prepared to say something she was glad her grandmother wasn't alive to hear. Or her mother for that matter. 'I'm…pregnant.'

There were a few astounded seconds while Stella appeared to be having some difficulty digesting what she'd just been told. 'I wasn't aware you were seeing anyone,' she said at last, carefully. 'Have I missed something?'

And here it was. The horrible reality. Did she try to dress it up into acceptable bite-sized chunks so that her friend might understand? Tara wondered desperately. No, there wasn't a single chunk of this which could in any way be described as acceptable. In the end she managed to condense it down into a couple of bald sentences which she still found difficult to believe.

'I had sex with Lucas,' she said. 'And I'm expecting his baby.'

'You had sex with Lucas Conway?'

'I did.'

'You're kidding me?'

'I'm afraid I'm not.'

Stella shook her head from side to side, her thick black hair gleaming in the autumn afternoon sunshine. 'I wasn't even aware you fancied him!' she exclaimed, blinking at her in astonishment. 'Or that you were his type!'

'I didn't. And I'm not.'

'So what happened?'

Tara shrugged and the bitter taste in the back of her throat only intensified. 'I still can't quite work it out.'

'Well, *try*, Tara.'

Tara worried her teeth into her bottom lip before meeting her friend's incredulous gaze. 'He said something pretty mean to me, which focussed me into thinking I should get a new job.'

'Which I've been saying to you for ages,' said Stella darkly.

'He told me he didn't want me to leave—'

'Please don't tell me he *seduced* you so you'd change your mind?'

Tara shook her head. 'Of course he didn't. It wasn't like that.'

'Then just how was it, Tara?'

How could you put into words something which had flared between the two of them over dinner that evening? Something which had changed the way they were with each other, so they'd suddenly gone from being boss and employee to a man and a woman who were achingly aware of the other? Even if you could, it wasn't something you'd dare admit to a friend, for fear of coming over as slightly deranged—or even stupid. Both of which were probably true in her case. 'It just happened,' she said simply. 'I can't explain it.'

There was a pause and Stella's eyes bored into her. 'So now what happens?'

This was the question which really needed answering and Tara knew that there was no alternative than to face the thing she was dreading more than anything else.

'I'm going to have to go to New York and tell him.'

CHAPTER FIVE

THE WORLD AS he knew it had just come to
an end but Lucas kept his expression blank
as he finished reading the letter the attorney
had given him. It had shocked and sickened
him—the final sentence dancing before his
eyes—but somehow he kept it together. He
could feel the punch of his heart and the faint
clamminess at his brow, but his hands were
steady as he folded the piece of paper carefully and slipped it back inside the envelope.

'Do you have any queries, Mr Conway?'
the lawyer was asking him. 'Anything you'd
like to discuss with us, regarding the con-
tents?'

A million things, thought Lucas grimly—
and then some. But they were the kind of
questions which couldn't be answered by
some anonymous attorney he could see was
burning up with curiosity. Not when he could

manage to work out the most important bits for himself.

And suddenly it was as if a heavy mist had lifted and everything which made up the sometimes confusing landscape of his past suddenly become clear. It explained so many important things. Why his 'father' had always been so cruel to him and why his mother...

His mother.

He felt a twist of something which felt more like anger than pain as finally he understood why he'd never felt as if he belonged anywhere. *Because he didn't. His parents were not his parents and he was not the man he'd thought himself to be. Everything had changed in the time it took to read that letter.*

And yet nothing had changed, he reminded himself grimly. Not really. He was still Lucas Conway, not Lucas Gonzalez. A pulse flickered at his temple. And no way was he ever going to call himself Lucas Sabato, his birth name. He shook his head. He was the man he had set out to be. A truly self-made man.

'We had some difficulty tracking you down after your father's death,' the lawyer was saying smoothly. 'Given that you'd changed your name and settled in Europe. And given, of course, that you were estranged from your family.'

Behind his desk the man was looking at him with a hopeful expression, as if waiting for Lucas to put him out of his misery and reveal why he had been so keen to conceal his true identity for all these years. Lucas felt his mouth flatten.

Because he had no intention of enlightening the lawyer.

No intention of enlightening anyone.

Why should he? His inner life had always been his and his alone—his thoughts too dark to share. And they had just got a whole shade darker, he realised bitterly, before pushing them away with an ease born of habit. Much simpler to adopt the slick and sophisticated image he presented to the world—the one which discouraged people to dig beneath the surface. Because who in their right mind wanted to explore certain and unremitting pain?

Hadn't that been one of the unexpected advantages to becoming a billionaire at such an early age—that people were so dazzled by his wealth, they didn't stop to explore his past too deeply? Or rather, people became so obsequious when you were loaded, that *you* were able to control how you wanted conversations to play out. He was good at evasion and obfuscation. He didn't even tell people where he'd been born—sidestepping curious questions with the same deft touch which had enabled him to become one of the youngest billionaires in all Ireland. His accent had helped to obscure his background, too. It had been difficult to place—his cultured New York drawl practically ironed out by years of multilingual schooling in Switzerland. And Ireland had provided the final confusing note—with the soft, lilting notes he had inevitably picked up along the way.

'Thanks for all your help,' he said smoothly as he rose to his feet, tucking the envelope into the inside pocket of his jacket.

He was barely aware of the lawyer shaking his hand or the secretary outside who stood up and smoothed her pencil skirt over her shapely bottom as he passed by, her hopeful smile fading as he failed to stop by her desk. Outside he was aware of the faint chill in the air. The reminder that fall was upon them. After a busy couple of weeks of business meetings, things had looked very different this morning when he'd lined up another apartment viewing, intending to stay in the city for a minimum of six months. Yet there was no reason to change that plan, he reminded himself. No reason at all. He hadn't been back here in years because he hadn't wanted to run into his father, but the man who had erroneously claimed that title was now dead and he wasn't going to let that bastard reach out from beyond the grave and influence him any more. Why *not* reclaim the city of his youth and enjoy it as he had never been able to do before?

With a quick glance at his watch, he set off by foot to meet the real-estate agent. He walked along Fifth Avenue, his body tensing as he stared up at the Flatiron building he hadn't seen since he'd been, what…fourteen? Fifteen? That had been the last time he'd spent his school vacation here. That particular homecoming had ended in the usual violence when his father had raised his fist to him but Lucas had turned his back and simply walked away, trying to block out the sound of the other's man's taunts which had been ringing in his ears.

'Not man enough to fight?'

It had been a flawed assessment because for the first time ever, Lucas had felt too *much* of a man to fight back. He'd filled out that summer and his muscles had been hard and strong. The almost constant sport he'd done at his fancy Swiss boarding school had made him into a fine athlete and deep down he knew he could have taken out his adoptive father, Diego Gonzalez, with a single swipe.

And the reason he hadn't was that because he was afraid once he started, he wouldn't know when to stop. That he would keep punching and punching the cruel bully who had made his life such a misery.

So he had carried on walking and not looked back. The only other time he had returned had been for his mother's funeral, when the two men had sat on opposite sides of the church without speaking. With the cloying scent of white lilies making him want to retch, Lucas remembered staring at the ornate scrolling on the lavish coffin, realising he'd never really known the woman he'd thought at the time had given birth to him. And he had been right, hadn't he? He hadn't known her at all.

But he wasn't going to dwell on that. He had spent his life rejecting the past and he wasn't going to change that now.

Deliberately focussing his attention on the here and now, he saw a woman standing up at the lights in front of him and the tawny colour of her hair made him think about Tara, even though that was something else he had decided was off-limits. He'd told himself that it had been a mistake. That maybe it had happened because he'd been thrown off-balance by what had lain ahead of him in New York. But at least he had let her down gently and no real harm had been done. And as she'd said herself—she'd had to lose her virginity some time.

Yet his eagerness to put her out of his mind hadn't been the plain sailing he'd expected. His night-time dreams had been haunted by memories of her slim, pale body and the delicious tightness he'd encountered as he had entered her. He would wake up frustrated and angry—with a huge erection throbbing uncomfortably between his thighs.

He still couldn't quite believe he'd had sex with her—his innocent housekeeper. Someone who, despite her fiery curls, had always seemed to blend into the background of his life, so that he hadn't regarded her as a woman at all—just someone to cook and clean and scrub for him. But she'd been a woman that night in his bed, hadn't she? All milky limbs and hair which had glowed like fire as the storm had flashed through the sky with an elemental force which had seemed to mimic what had been taking place in his bed. He found himself recalling the passion with which she'd kissed him and the eagerness with which she'd fallen into his arms. And then the unbelievable realisation—of discovering he was her first and only lover.

How could he have been so reckless?

His uncomfortable preoccupation was interrupted by the vibration of the cell-phone in his pocket and when he pulled it out his fingers froze around the plastic rectangle as he saw the name which had flashed up onto the screen. He shook his head in slight disbelief, as if his thoughts had somehow managed to conjure up her presence.

Tara.

Quickly, he calculated the time in Dublin and frowned. Getting on for ten in the evening, when normally she would have been laying the table for his breakfast, before retiring to her room at the top of the house. Of course, he wasn't there to make breakfast for, so she was free to do whatever she wanted, but that wasn't the point. The point was that she was ringing him.

Why was she ringing him?

He couldn't think of a conversation they could possibly have which wouldn't be excruciatingly uncomfortable, but, despite wanting to let the call go to voicemail, he knew he couldn't ignore her. He might wish he could take back that night and give it a different outcome but that wasn't possible. And she'd been a faithful employee for many years, hadn't she? Didn't he owe her a couple of minutes of conversation, even if it was going to be something of an ordeal? What if there'd been a burglary—a bone fide one this time, not just some holy statue crashing to the floor in the middle of a storm?

He felt an unmistakable wave of guilt as his thumb hit the answer button. 'Tara!' he said, his voice unnaturally bright, and he thought how usually he would have greeted such a call with a faint growl—the underlying message that he hoped she had a good reason for ringing. 'This is a surprise!'

'Is it a bad time to ring?'

She sounded nervous. Maybe she was remembering that other time when she'd called him and he'd been abroad, with a model called Catkin. Despite the warning look he'd given her, Catkin had picked up his phone and answered it, her voice laughing and smoky with sex. He remembered Tara's stuttering embarrassment when she'd finally come on the line and the way the model had sniggered beside him, loud enough to be heard. And with that loathsome demonstration of feminine cruelty, she had unwittingly put an end to their relationship.

'I'm dodging pedestrians on Fifth Avenue, Tara,' he said lightly. 'So you may have trouble hearing me above all the traffic noise.'

'Oh.'

She sounded flat now and he thought how their easy familiarity seemed to have been replaced by an odd new formality as he asked a question which sounded more dutiful than caring. 'Nothing's wrong, I hope?'

Her response was cautious. As if she was picking out her words—like someone sorting through the loose change in their pocket while searching for a two-euro coin. 'Not exactly.'

Not exactly? What the hell was that supposed to mean? *Please don't start telling me that you miss me or that—God forbid— you've decided you're in love with me.* 'No burst pipes in the basement?' he enquired, his forced joviality not quite hitting the mark.

'No, nothing like that. Lucas, I have… I have to talk to you.'

He could feel his heart sink because this sounded exactly as he'd feared. He'd had too many of these conversations in the past with women unable to recognise that their needs were very different. That the sex they'd shared meant nothing—it was just sex. She probably wanted to see him again, and soon—while he most definitely wanted to close the page on it. 'I thought that's exactly what we *were* doing,' he said smoothly.

'No. I don't mean a phone call. I mean face to face!' she burst out, her voice tinged with a desperation he'd never heard there before.

'But I'm in New York, Tara,' he told her, almost gently, because if he was going to have to let her down—which he suspected he was—then he needed to be kind about it. Because wasn't it his own damned fault that his housekeeper was now clearly pining for him? 'And you're in Dublin.'

'No, I'm not,' she corrected, sounding a little more confident now. 'I've just flown into LaGuardia.'

'LaGuardia?' he echoed incredulously. 'You mean you're in New York?'

'Obviously.' Her voice became terse.

Afterwards Lucas would wonder how he could have been so stupid, but that was only afterwards, when the hard, cold facts had finally percolated into his disbelieving brain. Maybe it was the double whammy of finding out the truth about his parentage which had sucked all the sense and perception out of him. Which meant he was able to shelve the glaringly obvious reason why Tara Fitzpatrick had taken it into her head to follow him to America, and to give a nod of acknowledgement to the curvy real-estate agent who had appeared outside the main entrance of the apartment block.

'Look, I haven't got time for this now, Tara. I'm meeting someone. Hi, Brandy,' he said, forcing a smile before putting his mouth close to the phone and hissing into it. 'Can you take a cab from the airport?'

'Of course I can!' She sounded angry now. 'I'm not a complete fool.'

'Meet me in the bar of the Meadow Hotel at seven. We can talk then.'

He cut the call and walked up the stairs towards the elegant town house, where the agent was slanting him a great big smile.

CHAPTER SIX

DESPITE ALL HER BRAVADO, Tara wondered if
Lucas had deliberately chosen to meet her in
the most inaccessible bar in New York. It was
situated deep in the bowels of the fanciest
hotel she could ever have imagined—a place
which instantly made her feel overheated,
overdressed and scruffy. She'd worn a thick
sweater with her jeans because it was autumn
and the city was supposed to be colder than
Dublin—but the temperature inside the hotel
made it feel more like summer and conse-
quently there were little beads of sweat already appearing on her brow and stubborn
curls were sticking to the back of her neck,
like glue. And she couldn't take the sweater
off because she had only a very old vest top
on underneath.

After convincing the granite-faced door-
man that her appointment was genuine, she

was instructed to put her anorak and old suitcase in the cloakroom, where she was given a
look of frank disbelief by the attendant. Her
long scarf she kept draped round her neck out
of habit, like an overaged child still clutching
a security blanket. Tucking her ticket into her
purse, she walked through the huge foyer—
past impossibly thin women on impossibly
high heels who were smiling adoringly into
the faces of much older men—and never had
she felt quite so awkward. Several times she
had to ask for directions and was made to
feel even more self-conscious for not knowing where she was going. As if showing any
kind of ignorance meant you'd failed a test
you hadn't even realised you were taking.

Eventually she found the bar, which was
situated down a dimly lit passageway—dimly
lit and daunting with its understated display
of quiet opulence and a lavish oriental feel.
Standing in front of a display of coloured
glasses and bottles, a barman was vigorously
shaking a cocktail mixture as if it were a pair
of maracas, playing to the group of business-
men sitting on tall stools at the bar in front
of him. It was definitely a man's room but
Tara was met with nothing but disparaging
glances, indicating that without the clothes,

the sophistication or the glamour, she was the wrong kind of woman to drink in a place like this. And didn't that simple fact acknowledge more clearly than words ever could just how awful the predicament in which she now found herself?

Where *was* Lucas? she thought, with a tinge of desperation as she sat down at a vacant table in the corner of the room and snuck a glance at her watch. And who was this woman called Brandy he'd been meeting when she'd telephoned him from the airport? She felt her self-esteem take another dramatic nose-dive as a familiar voice broke into her reverie.

'Tara?'

Thank heavens. Her heart pounded with relief. It was Lucas and he must have entered the room without her noticing because he was standing right beside her. She could detect his subtle scent as his shadow enveloped her, making her acutely aware of his powerful body. As befitted the sophisticated environment, he was wearing a suit, a crisp shirt and a tie—but, despite the elegant exterior, Tara knew all too well what lay beneath the sophisticated city clothes.

And suddenly he was no longer her soon-to-be ex-boss who had migrated to the opposite side of the globe, but the man with whom she'd shared all kinds of intimacies. The man with whom she had lain naked—skin next to warm and quivering skin. Who had stroked her eager body with infinite precision and licked his tongue over her puckering nipples. Had she really lost her virginity to the man she'd worked for and never looked twice at for all those years? Had he really thrust deep inside her as he'd taken her innocence and introduced her to that terrible and exquisite joy? How did something like that even *happen*?

Her heart began to race even faster. It was one thing being in Dublin and deciding that telling him to his face was the only way to impart her unwanted news—but now she wondered if she had been too hasty. Should she have sent him an email, or a text, even though it would have been an extremely impersonal method of communicating that she was carrying his baby? Suddenly what she was about to tell him seemed unbelievable— especially here, in this setting. Because this was his world, not hers. It was quietly moneyed and privileged—and it was pretty obvious that she stuck out like some country hick with her home-knitted scarf and cheap jeans.

'H-hello, Lucas,' she said.

'Tara.'

His voice was non-committal as he gave a brief nod of recognition, but as he turned to look at her properly Tara almost reeled back in shock because his face looked *ravaged*—there was no other word for it. The faint lines which edged his mouth seemed deeper—as if someone had coloured them in with a charcoal pencil. And despite the dim golden glow cast out by the tall light nearby, she could detect a bleak emptiness in his green eyes. As if the Lucas she knew had been replaced by someone else—a cool and indifferent stranger, but one who was radiating a quiet and impenetrable fury. Lucas was no even-tempered, angelic boss, but she'd never seen him looking like this before. What was responsible for such a radical change? Was he angry that she'd turned up without warning and was this to be her punishment—being given the ultimate cold shoulder for daring to confront him like this?

Well, his reaction was just too bad and she wasn't going to let it get to her. She couldn't afford to. She wasn't some desperate ex-lover chasing him to the far ends of the earth because she couldn't accept their relationship was over, but the woman who was carrying his baby. She needed to do this and she would do it with dignity.

'I know this is unexpected.'

'You can say that again.' He sat down opposite her, loosening his tie as he did so, but his powerful body remained tense as he looked at her. 'Have you ordered yourself a drink?'

Now was not the time to explain that she'd been too intimidated by the ambidextrous barman to dare to open her mouth, aligned with the very real fear that buying something here would eat dangerously into her limited budget. 'Not yet.'

'Would you like to try one of their signature cocktails?' He fixed her with an inquiring look and she knew him well enough to recognise that his smile was forced. 'They come with their own edible umbrella and are something of an institution.'

She tried not to look ungrateful, even though she found his tone distinctly patronising. But he was summoning a waitress who was travelling at the speed of light in her eagerness to serve him and Tara told herself not to be unreasonable. She had to look at it from his point of view. They'd had some bizarre unplanned sex and now it must look as if she were trying to gatecrash his new life. Because he still didn't know why she was here and what she was about to tell him—and it was going to come as a huge shock when he did.

So the sooner she did it, the better.

Nervously, she cleared her throat. 'Just a glass of water would be fine for me.'

The darkness on his face intensified, as if he had suddenly picked up on some of the tension which was making her push nervously at the cuticles of her fingernails, like someone giving themselves a makeshift manicure. He glanced up at the eager server who was hovering around his chair. 'Bring us a bottle of sparkling water, will you?'

'Coming right up, sir.'

And once they were on their own, all pretence was gone. The courteous civility he'd employed when asking her what she wanted to drink had all but disappeared. All that was left in its place was a flintiness which was intimidating and somehow *scary*, because it suddenly felt as if the man sitting opposite was a complete stranger, and Tara shifted uncomfortably on the velvet seat, dreading what she had to tell him.

'So. I'm all ears. Are you going to tell me why you're here, Tara?' Those curiously empty green eyes fixed her with a quizzical look. 'Why you've made such a dramatic unannounced trip?'

Tara sucked in a deep breath, wishing that the water had arrived so that she could have refreshed her parched mouth before she spoke. Wishing there were some other way to say it. She sucked a hot breath into her lungs and expelled it on a shudder. 'I'm… I'm having a baby,' she croaked.

There was a silence. A long silence which even eclipsed Stella's reaction when she'd told her the news. Tara watched Lucas's face go through a series of changes. First anger and then a shake of the head, which was undoubtedly denial. She wondered if he would try bargaining with her before passing through stages of depression and acceptance—all of which she knew were the five stages of grief.

'You can't be,' he said harshly.

Tara nodded. This was grief, all right. 'I'm afraid I am.'

'You can't be,' he repeated, leaning forward so that his lowered voice was nothing more than a deep hiss of accusation. 'I used protection.'

Tara licked her lips, pleased when the server arrived with their bottle to interrupt their combat, although the silence grew interminably long as she poured the water and it fizzed and foamed over two ice-filled crystal glasses. It was only when the woman had gone and Tara had forced herself to gather her composure long enough to take a deep and refreshing mouthful that she nodded. 'I realise that. And I also understand that the barrier method isn't a hundred per cent reliable.'

Incredulously, he looked at her. 'The *barrier* method?' he echoed. 'Who the hell calls it that any more?'

'I read it in a book about pregnancy.'

'When was it published? Some time early in the eighteenth century?'

Tara urged herself to ignore his habitual sarcasm, which right now seemed more wounding than it had ever done before. This was way too important to allow hurt feelings and emotions to get in the way of what really mattered, which was the tiny life growing inside her. But neither was she prepared to just sit there and allow Lucas to hurl insults at her, not when he was as much to blame as she was. *And I don't want to feel blame,* she thought brokenly. *I don't want my baby to have all the judgmental stuff hurled at it which I once had to suffer.*

She put her glass down on the table with a shaky hand and the ice cubes rattled like wind chimes. 'Being flippant isn't going to help matters.'

'Really? So do you have a magic formula for something which *is* going to help matters, because if so I'm longing to hear it?'

'There's no need to be so...*rude!*'

He leaned forward so that the tiny pulse working frantically at his temple was easily visible. 'I'm not being rude, I'm being honest. I never wanted children, Tara,' he gritted out. 'Never. Do you understand? Not from when I was a teenage boy—and that certainty hasn't diminished one iota over the years.'

She told herself to stay calm. 'It wasn't exactly on my agenda either,' she said. 'But we're not talking hypothetical. This is real and I'm pregnant and I thought you had a right to know. That's all.'

Lucas stared at her, half wondering if she was going to suddenly burst out laughing and giggle, *'April Fool,'* and he would be angry at first, but ultimately relieved. He might even consider taking her up to his hotel room and exacting a very satisfying form of retribution—something which would give him a brief respite from the dark reality which had been visited upon him in that damned lawyer's office. But this was October, not April, and Tara wouldn't be insane enough to fly out here without warning unless what she said was true. And she wasn't smiling.

He thought about the ways in which he could react to her unwanted statement.

He could demand she take a DNA test and quiz her extensively about subsequent lovers she might have dallied with after he'd taken her innocence. But even as he thought it he knew only a fool would react in that way, because deep down he knew there had been no lover in Tara Fitzpatrick's life but him.

He could have a strong drink.

Maybe he would—because the time it took to slowly sip at a glass of spirit would give him time to consider his response to her. But not here. Not with half of New York City's movers and shakers in attendance and a couple of people he recognised staring at him curiously from the other side of the room. He wasn't surprised at their expressions, because never had anyone looked more as if they shouldn't be there than Tara Fitzpatrick, with her thick green sweater the colour of Irish hills and her striking hair piled on top of her head, with strands tumbling untidily down the sides of her pale face.

He saw that her ridiculously over-long scarf was wound around her neck—the multicoloured one she'd started knitting when she first came to work for him and which had once made him sarcastically enquire whether she ever planned to finish it. 'I don't know how to cast off,' had been her plaintive reply, and he had smiled before suggesting she ask someone. But he wasn't smiling now.

Was he ashamed of her? No. He'd broken enough rules in his own life to ever be described as a conformist and he didn't care that his skinny housekeeper was sporting a pair of unflattering jeans rather than a sleek cocktail dress like the few other women in the bar. And besides, hadn't he just discovered something about himself which would shock those onlookers in the bar and fill them with horror and maybe even a little pleasure at hearing about someone else's misfortune, if they knew the truth about him? The Germans even had a phrase for that, didn't they? Schadenfreude. That was it.

He needed to get away from these blood-red walls, which felt as if they were closing in on him, so he could try to make sense of what she'd told him. As if giving himself some time and space would lessen the anger and growing dread which were making his heart feel as heavy as lead.

'We can't talk here,' he ground out, rising to his feet. 'Come with me.'

She nodded obediently. Well, *of course* she would be obedient. Hadn't that been her role ever since she'd entered his life? To carry out his wishes and be financially recompensed for doing that—not to end up in his bed while he gave into an unstoppable passion which had seemed to come out of nowhere.

'Where are we going?' she questioned, once they'd exited the bar and were heading back down a dimly lit corridor towards the foyer.

'I have a room here in the hotel.'

'Lucas—'

'You can wipe that outraged look from your face,' he said roughly as he slowed down in front of the elevator. 'My mind is on far more practical things than sex, if that's what you're thinking.'

'Would you mind keeping your voice down?' she hissed.

'Isn't it a little late in the day for prudery, Tara?'

'I'm not being a prude,' she said, in a low voice. 'I just don't want every guest in this hotel knowing my business.'

He didn't trust himself to answer as he ushered her into the private elevator and hit the button for his suite. In tense and claustrophobic silence they rode to the top, his thoughts still spinning as he tried to come to grips with what she'd told him. But how could he possibly do that, when he'd meant what he said? He'd never wanted to be a father. Never. His experience of that particular relationship had veered from non-existent to violent—and he'd never had a loving mother to bail him out. At least now he knew the reason why, but that didn't make things any better, did it? In many ways it actually made them worse.

'In here,' he said tersely as the doors slid noiselessly open and they stepped into the penthouse suite of the Meadow Hotel, which was reputed to command one of the finest views of the Manhattan skyline. It was growing dark outside and already lights were twinkling like diamonds in the pale indigo sky. Most people would have automatically breathed their admiration on seeing such an unparalleled view of the city. But not Tara. She barely seemed to notice anything as she stood in the centre of the room and fixed those strange amber eyes on him.

'I came because I felt you had a right to know,' she began, as if she had prepared the words earlier.

'So you said in the bar.'

'And because I felt it better to tell you face to face,' she rushed on.

'But you didn't think to give me any warning?'

'How could I have done that without telling you what it was about?' She was quiet for a moment. 'I wanted to see your face when I told you.'

'And did my reaction disappoint you?'

'I'm a realist, Lucas. It was pretty much what I thought it would be.' She sucked in a deep breath. 'But I want you to know that this has nothing to do with any expectations on my part. I'm just giving you the facts, that's all. It's up to you what you do with them.'

Lucas flinched, suddenly aware of his heart's powerful reaction as he acknowledged he was to be a father. But it clenched in pain, not in joy. 'Brandy,' he said harshly. 'I'll order strong tea for you, but I think I need brandy.'

Her reaction was not what he'd been expecting. He'd thought she might be slightly pacified by him remembering the way she liked her tea—but instead she turned on him with unfamiliar fury distorting her face. 'Can't you leave your girlfriend out of it for a minute?' she flared. 'Can't we at least have this discussion in private without you talking to her?'

'Excuse me?' He narrowed his eyes. 'I'm afraid you've lost me, Tara. I haven't a clue what you're talking about.'

'You were meeting someone called Brandy when I called you from the airport!' she accused.

It might have been funny if it hadn't been so serious but Lucas was in no mood for laughing. 'That's the name of the house agent, not my girlfriend,' he gritted out, but her chance remark put him even more on his guard. Was she already showing signs of sexual jealousy? Already planning some kind of mutual future which would be a disaster for them both, despite her fiery words to the contrary? Well, the sooner he disabused her of that idea, the better. 'The drinks can wait. Why don't you take a seat over there, Tara?'

Tara didn't want to take a seat. She wanted to be back at home in her iron-framed bed in Dublin, where she could see the sweep of the

Irish sea in its ever-changing guises. Except that it *wasn't* her home, she reminded herself painfully—it was Lucas's. She bit her lip. But it was the closest she'd ever come to finding a place where she felt safe and settled—far away from all the demons of the past. 'I'd prefer to stand, if it's all right by you,' she said stiffly. 'I've been sitting on a long flight for hours and I need to stretch my legs.'

He nodded but she couldn't miss the faint trace of frustration which briefly hardened his eyes. Was he finding it difficult to cope with the fact that, since she was no longer technically his employee, he could no longer order her around as he wanted?

'As you wish,' he said. His drink seemingly forgotten, he stared at her. 'So where do we go from here?'

She wished he would show more of the emotion she'd seen in the bar a little while ago. It might have been mostly anger and negativity but at least it was *some* kind of feeling—not this icy and remote person who seemed nothing like the Lucas Conway she knew.

But she didn't know him, did she? Not really. And not just because he kept so much of himself hidden that people called him a closed book. You couldn't really know someone you worked for—not properly—because their interactions had only ever been superficial. Yes, she'd witnessed different sides of his character over the years—but ultimately she'd just been a person on his payroll and that meant he'd treated her like an employee, not an equal.

Had he ever treated his girlfriends as equals? she wondered. Judging by the things she'd witnessed over the years she would say that, no, he had not. If you were heavily into equality, you didn't pacify dumped exes by giving them expensive diamond necklaces rather than an explanation of what had gone wrong. *And you are not his girlfriend,* Tara reminded herself bitterly. *You are just a woman he had sex with and now you're carrying his baby.*

His baby.

Her fingers crept to touch her still-concave belly and she saw him follow the movement with the watchful attention of a cheetah she'd once seen on a TV wildlife programme, just before it pounced on some poor and unsuspecting prey.

'How…pregnant are you?' he questioned, lifting that empty gaze to her face.

He said the word *pregnant* like someone trying out a new piece of vocabulary, which was rather ironic given that he was such a remarkable linguist. And Tara found herself wanting to tell him that it felt just as strange for her. That she was as mixed up and scared and uncertain about the future as he must be. But she couldn't admit to that because she needed to be strong. Strong for her baby as well as for herself. She wasn't going to show weakness because she didn't want him to think she was throwing herself in front of him and asking for anything he wasn't prepared to give.

'It's still very early. Seven weeks.'

'And you're certain?'

'I did a test.'

'A reliable test?'

Silently, she counted to ten. 'I didn't buy some dodgy kit at the cut-price store, if that's what you're hinting at, Lucas. I'm definitely pregnant.'

'Have you seen a doctor?'

She hesitated. 'No. Not yet.' Would it sound ridiculous to tell him that she'd baulked at going to see the friendly family doctor in Dalkey—himself a grandfather—terrified of how she was going to answer when he asked her about the father of her baby? Terrified he would judge her, as people seemed to have been doing all her life.

She watched as Lucas walked over to the cocktail cabinet—a gleaming affair of beaten gold and shiny chrome—but he seemed to think better of it and turned back to face her, that remote expression still making his face look stony and inaccessible.

'So what do we do next?' He raised his dark brows. 'Any ideas? You must have had something in mind when you flew all this way to tell me. You want to have this baby, I take it?'

Tara screwed her face up as a blade of anger spiked into her and for a moment she actually thought she might burst into tears. 'Of course I want this baby!' she retaliated. 'What kind of a woman wouldn't want her baby?'

She wondered what had caused that look of real pain to cross his face and thought it ironic that if they had some of the closeness of real lovers, she might have asked him. But they weren't *real* lovers. They were just two people who had let passion get the better of them and were having to deal with the consequences.

'So is it a wedding ring you're after?' he enquired caustically. 'Is that it?'

'I've no desire to marry someone who finds it impossible to conceal his disgust at such a prospect!'

'I can't help the way I feel, Tara. I'm not going to lie. I told you I never wanted children,' he gritted out. 'And the logical follow-on from that is that I never wanted marriage either.'

'I didn't come here for either of those things,' she defended. 'But at least now I know exactly where I stand.' Her fingers tightened around the strap of her bag, which was still tied diagonally across her chest like a school satchel—in case anyone had tried to mug her. 'And since I've done what I set out to do, I'll be on my way.'

'Oh, really?' Dark eyebrows shot up and were hidden by his tousled dark hair. 'And where do you think you're going?'

She drew her shoulders back proudly. 'Back to Dublin, of course.'

He shook his head. 'You can't go back to Dublin.'

'Oh, I think you'll find I can do anything I please, Lucas Conway,' she answered, and for the first time in many hours she actually found comfort in a sense of her own empowerment. 'And you can't stop me.'

But it was funny how sometimes your own body could rebel and that you had no idea what was going on inside you. Maybe it was the economy flight which had been extremely cramped, or perhaps it had something to do with the dreadful food she'd been served during that journey, which she personally wouldn't have given to a dog. Add to that her see-sawing hormones and troubled emotions and no wonder that a sudden powerful wave of nausea washed over her.

Did her face blanch? Was that why Lucas stepped forward, an unfamiliar look of concern creasing his face as he reached out towards her? 'Tara? Are you okay?'

There was no delicate way to say it, even though it was an intimacy she had no desire to share with a man who'd shown her not one iota of compassion or respect since she'd got here.

She swayed like a blade of grass in the wind. 'I think I'm going to be sick!' she gasped.

He muttered something in French—or was it Italian?—and Tara moaned in dismay as he caught hold of her before she fell, lifting her up into his arms. Last time he'd carried her it had been a shortcut to his bed—and hadn't that been the beginning of all this trouble?—but this time he merely carried her to the nearest bathroom so she could give into the intense nausea which was gripping her. And as she bent over the bowl and started to retch he was still there, brushing away the curls which were dangling around her face, even though she tried to push him away with her elbow.

'G-go away,' she gasped, mortified.

'I'm not going anywhere.'

'I don't want you seeing me like this.'

'Don't worry about it, Tara,' he drawled. 'I've been on enough school football trips to have witnessed plenty of boys being sick.'

'It's not the same,' she moaned.

'Stop talking.'

She did but it took a while before she felt better-which was presumably why she allowed Lucas to dab at her face with a deliciously cool cloth. Then, after a moment of cold, hard scrutiny, he handed her some paste and a spare toothbrush.

'Wash up and take as long as you like. Call me if you need me. I'll be right outside.'

Tara waited until he had closed the bathroom door behind him, and as she staggered to her feet to the mirror she looked in horror at the white-faced reflection staring back at her. Her eyes were huge and haunted and her hair couldn't have been more of a mess, which was saying something. She tugged at the elastic band so that her curls tumbled free and shook her head impatiently.

What had she *done*?

Thrown up in front of a man who didn't want her here. Given him news he didn't want, a fact which he'd made no attempt to hide. Even worse, she was thousands of miles from home.

Past caring about her old vest top, she peeled off her too-hot sweater, splashed her face with water and then vigorously washed her hands until the suds stopped being grey. Then she brushed her teeth until they were minty-fresh and removed a hotel comb from its little packet of cellophane. It was slightly too small to properly attack her awry curls but she managed to marginally tame them before going over to the door. Whatever happened, she would cope, she thought grimly. Look what her mother and her granny had done during times when having a baby out of wedlock was the worst thing which could happen to a woman. She dug her teeth into her lip. It was true that their lives had been pretty much wrecked by circumstances but they had *managed*. And she would manage too.

Pushing open the door, she found Lucas waiting outside, his body tense and his features still dark with something which may have been concern but was underpinned with something much darker.

His question was dutiful rather than concerned. 'How are you feeling?'

'Better now,' she informed him stiffly.

'I'll ring for the doctor.'

'Please don't bother. I don't need a doctor, Lucas. Women often get sick when they're pregnant. I'd just like you to call me a cab and I'll stay in the hostel I've booked for tonight—and tomorrow I'll see about getting the first flight back to Ireland.'

He shook his head and now there was a look of grim resolution in his eyes. 'I'm afraid that's not going to happen, Tara.'

She tilted her chin in disbelieving challenge. 'You mean you're going to physically stop me?'

'If I need to, I will—because I would be failing in my duty if I allowed you to travel around New York on your own tonight, especially in your condition,' he agreed grimly. 'There's only one place you're going right now and that's to bed.'

'I'm not—'

'Oh, yes,' he said, in as firm a voice as she'd ever heard him use. 'You most certainly are. There's a guest suite right along the corridor. I've put your things in there. And it's pointless arguing, Tara. We both know that.'

Tara opened her mouth to object but he was right because she recognised that resolute light in Lucas's eyes of old. She'd seen it time and time again when he'd been in the middle of some big negotiation or trying to pull off a deal which nobody had believed could ever happen. Except that he made things happen. He had the wherewithal and the clout to mould people and events to his wishes. And didn't part of her *want* to lie down on a soft bed and close her eyes and shut out reality? To have sleep claim her so that maybe when she opened her eyes again she would feel better.

But how was that going to work and what could possibly make this situation better? She had let history repeat itself and she knew all too well the rocky road which lay ahead. But none of that bitter knowledge was a match against the fatigue which was seeping through her body and so she nodded her head in reluctant agreement. 'Oh, very well,' she mumbled ungratefully. 'You'd better show me the way.'

Lucas nodded, indicating the corridor which led to the guest accommodation, though he noticed she kept as far away from him as possible. Yet somehow her reluctance ignited a flicker of interest he wasn't prepared for and certainly didn't want. He frowned. Maybe it was because women didn't usually protest about staying in his hotel suite or try to keep him at arm's length like this. He was used to sustained adoration from ex-lovers, even though he was aware he didn't deserve such adoration. But women would do pretty much anything for a man with a big bank account who gave them plenty of orgasms, he thought cynically.

He'd tried to convince himself during the preceding weeks that the uncharacteristic lust he'd felt for Tara Fitzpatrick had gone. It *should* have gone by now. But to his surprise he realised it hadn't and he was discovering there was something about her which was still crying out to some atavistic need, deep inside him. Even when she was in those ill-fitting jeans and a vest top, he couldn't help thinking about her agile body. The pale breasts and narrow hips. The golden brush of freckles which dusted her skin. He remembered the way he had lowered her down onto his rocky hardness and that split-second when he had met the subtle resistance of her hymen. And yes, he had felt indignation that she hadn't told him—but hadn't that been quickly followed by a primitive wash of pleasure at the thought that he was her first and only lover?

His throat grew dry as he continued to watch her. The red curtain of curls was swaying down her back, reminding him of the way he'd run his fingers through their wild abundance, and the hot punch of desire which had hardened his groin now became almost unendurable.

Yet she was pregnant. His skin grew cold with a nameless kind of dread—a different kind of dread from the one he had experienced in the lawyer's office. She was carrying his child.

And in view of what he had learned today— wouldn't any child which had sprung from his loins have an unknown legacy?

He opened the bedroom door and saw the

unmistakable opening of her lips as her roving gaze drank in the unashamed luxury of her surroundings and it was a timely reminder that, despite her innocence, she was still a woman. And who was to say she wouldn't be as conniving as all other women, once she got into her stride? 'I hope it meets with your satisfaction,' he drawled. 'I think you'll find everything in here you need, Tara.'

Did she recognise the cynical note in his voice? Was that why she turned a defiant face up to his?

'I'm only staying the one night, mind.'

He wanted to tell her that she was mistaken, but for once Lucas kept his counsel. Let her sleep, he thought grimly—and by morning he would have decided what their fate was to be.

CHAPTER SEVEN

TARA OPENED HER eyes and for a moment she thought she'd died and gone to heaven. She was lying in a bed—the most comfortable bed she'd ever slept in—in a room which seemed composed mostly of huge windows. Windows to the front of her and windows to the side, all looking out onto the fairy-tale skyline of New York. She blinked as she levered herself up onto her elbows. Like giant pieces of Lego, the tall buildings soared up into the cloudless October sky and looked almost close enough to touch. Sitting up properly, she leaned back against the feathery bank of pillows and looked around some more—because last night she'd been too dazed and tired to take in anything much.

It was…amazing, she conceded. The ceiling was made of lacquered gold, the floors of polished parquet, so that everything around her seemed to gleam with a soft and precious life. On an exquisite writing desk stood a vase of pure white orchids so perfect that they almost didn't look real. And there, in one corner of the room, was her battered old suitcase, looking like a scruffy intruder in the midst of all this opulence.

She flinched.

Just like her, really.

Lucas must have put a glass of water on the bedside table and she reached out and gulped most of it down thirstily. On slightly wobbly legs she got out of bed and found the en-suite bathroom—a monument to marble and shiny chrome—and, after freshening up and brushing her hair, thought about going to find Lucas. She needed to talk about returning to Ireland and he needed to realise that she meant it and he couldn't keep her here by force. But her legs were still wobbly and the bed was just too tempting and so she climbed back in beneath the crisp sheets and before she knew it was dozing off.

She was woken by the sensation of someone else being in the room and her eyelids fluttered open to find Lucas standing beside the bed, staring down at her. His jaw was unshaven and the faint shadows shading the skin beneath his vivid green eyes made it look as if he hadn't had a lot of sleep. Black jeans hugged his narrow hips and long legs and his soft grey shirt was unbuttoned at the neck, offering a tantalising glimpse of the butter-scotch-coloured skin beneath. Tara swallowed. It should have felt weird to have her one-time boss standing beside her bed while she lay beneath the duvet wearing nothing more than a baggy T-shirt, but somehow it didn't feel weird at all.

This is my new normal, she thought weakly. The same normal which was making her breasts sting with awareness as her gaze roved unwillingly over his powerful body. *Because this man has known you intimately,* she realised. *Known you in a way nobody else has ever done.* She felt a clench of exquisitely remembered desire, low in her belly, and before she could stop them vivid images began to flood her mind as she remembered how it felt to encase him—big and hard and erect. Despite everything she'd been brought up to believe, it hadn't felt shameful at all. It had felt *right*. As if she hadn't known what it really meant to be alive and to be a woman—until Lucas Conway had entered her and she'd given that little gasp as brief pain had morphed into earth-shattering pleasure.

Her heart was thumping so hard she was afraid he might notice its fluttering movement beneath her T-shirt and so she sat up, her fingers digging into the duvet, which she dragged up to a deliberately demure level, just below her chin. Only then was she ready to give him a cautious nod. 'Good morning.'

He returned the nod but didn't return the sentiment. 'Did you sleep well?'

'Very well, thank you.'

'Good.'

They stared at each other cautiously, like two strangers forced into close proximity. Tara cleared her throat, wishing she could get rid of the sense of there being an unexploded time bomb ticking away unseen in one corner of the room. But maybe that was what babies really were. She forced her attention to the pale sunlight which splashed over the wooden floor. 'Is it late?'

'Just after eleven.'

'Right.' Her fingers didn't relax their hold on the duvet. 'I need to start thinking about leaving—and it's no good shaking your head like that, because I don't work for you any more, Lucas. You can't just tell me no and expect me to fall in with your wishes, just because that's what I've always done before.'

His eyes narrowed and she saw the hard light of the practised negotiator enter them, turning them into flinty jade colour. 'I wouldn't dream of laying down the law—'

'You've had a sudden personality change, have you?'

He completely ignored her interjection, and didn't respond to the humour which was intended. 'We need to talk about where we go from here,' he continued. 'Just hear me out, will you, Tara?'

Once again she shifted awkwardly but the movement didn't manage to shift the syrupy ache between her thighs, which was making her wish that he would tumble down on top of her.

And where did that come from?

Since when had she become so preoccupied with sex?

She swallowed.

Since the night Lucas Conway had introduced her to it.

With an effort she dragged her thoughts back to the present, wondering why he was talking so politely. He must want something very badly, she thought, instantly on her guard. 'Okay,' she said.

He traced his thumb over the dark shadow at his jaw, drawing her unwilling attention to its chiselled contours. 'Would you like coffee first?'

'I'm not drinking coffee at the moment, thank you. I've already had some water and I think you're playing for time. So why don't you just cut to the chase and tell me what's on your mind, Lucas?'

Lucas's jaw tightened with frustration. It was easy to forget that she'd been working for him and sharing his house for years. Longer than he'd lived with anyone at a single stretch—and that included his parents. But despite the relative longevity of their relationship, Tara didn't really *know* him—not deep down. Nobody did. He made sure of that because he'd been unwilling to reveal the dark emptiness inside him, or the lack of human connection which had always made him feel disconnected from the world. Now he understood what had made him the man he was. He'd been given a kind of justification for his coldness and his lack of empathy—but that was irrelevant. He wasn't here to focus on his perceived failings. He was here to try to find a solution to an unwanted problem.

'You don't have any family, do you, Tara?'

She flinched. 'No. I told you at my interview that my grandmother brought me up after my mother died, and my grandmother has also since passed.'

Lucas nodded. Had she? He hadn't bothered probing much beyond that first interview, because if you asked someone personal questions, there was always the danger they might just ask them back. And Tara had impressed him with her work ethic and the fact that, physically, he hadn't found her in the least bit distracting. *What a short-sighted fool he had been.*

Because the truth was that she was looking pretty distracting right now—with those wild waves of hair bright against the whiteness of the pillow and her amber eyes strangely mesmeric as they surveyed him from beneath hooded eyelids.

'Why don't you put some clothes on?' he said, shooting the words out like bullets. 'And we'll have this discussion over breakfast.'

'Okay.' Tara nodded, not wanting to say that she didn't feel like breakfast—just relieved he had turned his back and was marching out of the room, wanting to be free of the terrible *awareness* which had crept over her skin as his green gaze had skated over her in that brooding and sultry way.

After showering and shrugging on an enormous bathrobe, she found him drinking coffee in the wood-panelied dining room— another room which was dominated by the Manhattan skyline and she was glad of the distraction.

'I can't believe the size of this place,' she said, walking over to the window and looking down at a green corner of what must have been Central Park. 'Why, even the bathroom is bigger than the hostel Stella and I stayed in last Christmas!'

'I'm not really interested in hearing how you saw New York on a budget,' he drawled. 'Just sit down and eat some breakfast, will you?'

As she turned around Tara was about to suggest it might do him good to stay in the kind of cramped accommodation which *most* people had to contend with, but then she saw a big trolley covered with silver domes which she hadn't noticed before. On it was a crystal jug of juice, a basket covered by a thick linen napkin, and on a gilded plate were little pats of butter—as yellow as the buttercups which used to grow in the fields around Ballykenna. She'd thought she wasn't hungry but her growling stomach told her otherwise and she realised how long it had been since she'd had a square meal. And she'd been sick last night, she reminded herself.

She walked towards the trolley to help herself but Lucas stayed her with an imperious wave of his hand.

'No. I don't want you collapsing on me again,' he instructed tersely. 'Sit down and I'll serve you.'

Tara opened her mouth to tell him she was perfectly capable of serving herself, but then a perverse sense of enjoyment crept over her as he offered cereal and eggs, fruit and yoghurt, and she sat there helping herself with solid silver spoons. Because if she allowed herself to forget her awful dilemma for a moment, this really *was* role reversal at its most satisfying! The food was delicious but she ate modestly, a fact which didn't escape Lucas's notice.

'No wonder you always look as if a puff of wind could blow you away,' he observed caustically. 'You don't eat enough.'

She buttered a slice of toast. 'My book on

pregnancy says little and often if you want to try to avoid nausea.'

'Just how many books on pregnancy are you reading just now?'

'As many as I need. I know nothing about motherhood and I want to be as well prepared as possible.'

Wincing deeply, he sucked in a lungful of air. 'You say you want this baby—'

'I don't just *say* it. Lucas—I mean it,' she declared fiercely. 'And if for one moment you're daring to suggest—'

'I wasn't suggesting anything,' he cut across her, his expression darkening. 'And before you fly off the handle, let me make my views plain, just so there can be no misunderstanding. Which is that I'm glad you've chosen to carry this child and not...'

'Not what?' Tara questioned in bewilderment as his mouth twisted.

'It doesn't matter,' he snarled.

'Oh, I think it does.' She drew in a deep breath, putting her napkin down and realising almost impartially that her fingers were trembling. 'Look, we're not the same as we used to be, are we? We're no longer boss and employee.' She looked at him earnestly. 'I'm not sure how you'd define our relationship now—the only thing I'm sure about is that we're going to be parents and that means we need to be honest with each other. I'm not expecting you to say things you don't mean, Lucas, but I am expecting you to tell me the truth.'

The truth. The words sounded curiously threatening as they washed over him and Lucas stared at her. For a man who had spent his life denying and concealing his feelings, her heartfelt appeal seemed like a step too far and his instinct was to stonewall her. Yet he recognised that this was like no other situation he'd ever found himself in. He couldn't just buy himself out of this, not unless he was prepared to throw a whole lot of money her way and tell her that he wanted to cut all ties with her and his unborn child for ever.

He would have been a liar if he'd said he wasn't tempted…

But how could he do that, given the bitter reality of his own history which had been revealed to him by that damned lawyer? Wouldn't that mean, in effect, that he was as culpable as his own mother had been?

And look how that had turned out.

'Have you given any thought to how you see your future?' he demanded.

Tara shook her head. 'Not really. Have you?'

'Finish your breakfast first.'

But Tara's mouth felt dry with nerves and it was difficult to force anything else down, especially under that seeking green gaze—and she noticed he hadn't touched anything himself except two cups of inky coffee. 'I've finished,' she said, dabbing at her lips with a heavy-duty linen napkin.

He placed the palms of his hands on the table in front of him, looking like a man who meant business. 'So,' he said, his emotionless gaze still fixed on her. 'It seems there are several options available to us. We just have to work out which is the most acceptable, to both of us.'

Tara nodded. 'Go ahead,' she said cautiously. 'I'm all ears.'

He nodded. 'Obviously I will provide for you and the baby, financially.'

'Do you want me to do a dance of joy around the room just because you're accepting responsibility?'

His frown deepened. 'It's not like you to be quite so…irascible, Tara.'

Tara didn't know what irascible meant but she could guess. Should she tell him her crankiness stemmed from fear about the future, despite his offer of financial support? Surely even Lucas could work that out for himself. She studied the obdurate set of his jaw. Maybe that was hoping for too much. He was probably thinking about his own needs, not hers. And suddenly she realised that she couldn't afford to be vulnerable and neither could she keep second-guessing him. She was responsible for the life she carried and she needed to be strong.

'Why don't we just stick to the matter in hand?' she questioned coolly. 'Tell me what you have in mind.'

Was he surprised by her sudden air of composure? Was that why he subjected her to a look of rapid assessment? It was a look Tara recognised all too well. It was his negotiating look.

'You have no family and…neither do I,' he said slowly. 'And since I'd already made plans to stay in New York for the next few months, I see no reason to change those plans, despite the fact that you're pregnant.'

She thought how cleverly he had defined the situation, making it sound as if the baby had nothing to do with him. But perhaps that was exactly how he saw it, and Tara certainly wasn't going to push him for answers. She was never going to beg him, not for anything. Nor push him into a corner. 'Go on,' she said calmly.

'You could stay here and return to Ireland in time for the birth,' he continued. 'That would free you from unwanted scrutiny— or the questions which would undoubtedly spring up if you went back home.'

And now the surreal sense of calm she'd been experiencing suddenly deserted her. Tara could feel colour flooding into her cheeks as she pushed back her chair and sprang to her feet, her hair falling untidily around her face. 'I see!' she said, her voice shaking with emotion as she pushed a thick wave over her shoulder. 'You're trying to hide me away in a country where nobody knows me! You're ashamed of me—is that it?'

'If there's any shame to be doled out, then it's me who should bear it,' he retorted, though he seemed mesmerised by her impatient attentions as she brushed away her unruly hair with a fisted hand. 'I was the one who took your virginity!'

Was it her pregnancy which made Tara feel so volatile? Which made her determined to redefine his view of what had happened that fateful night, because didn't his jaundiced summary of events *downgrade* it? Or was it simply that she had carried the burden of shame around for a whole lifetime and suddenly the weight was just too much to bear? 'I wasn't some *innocent victim* who just fell into the arms of an experienced philanderer,' she declared.

'Thanks for the uplifting character reference,' he said drily.

'That wasn't how it happened,' she continued doggedly. 'That night we were just…'

'Just what, Tara?' he prompted silkily.

She stared down at her bare feet for a moment before lifting her heavy-lidded gaze to his. 'We were just a man and woman who wanted each other and status didn't come into it—not yours, nor mine,' she whispered. 'Surely you're not going to deny that, Lucas?'

Lucas was taken aback by her candour and surprised by his response to it, because an emotional statement like that would usually have made him run for the hills. Maybe it was the naïve way she expressed herself which touched something deep inside him—something which unfurled the edges of the cold emptiness which had always seemed such an integral part of him. For a moment he felt almost...*exposed*—as if she were threatening to peel back a layer of his skin to see what lay beneath. And no way did he wish her to see the blackness of his soul.

So that when his groin grew rocky it felt almost like a reprieve, because wasn't it simpler to allow desire to flood him? To let lust quieten all those nebulous feelings he hadn't addressed since leaving the lawyer's office and which had been compounded by the bombshell Tara had dropped in his lap soon afterwards? He looked at the wild spill of her hair and her sleepy amber eyes. The towelling bathrobe she had pulled on was swamping her slender body in a way which should have been unflattering, but it only seemed to emphasise her fragility and suddenly he knew he wanted her again and he didn't care if it was wrong. Because the worst had already happened, hadn't it—what else could possibly eclipse the prospect of unwanted fatherhood?

Slowly yet purposefully, he walked across the dining room towards her and now her cat-like eyes weren't quite so sleepy. Their pupils had dilated so they looked night-dark against her pale skin.

'Lucas?' she questioned faintly. 'What do you think you're doing?'

'Oh, come on, Tara.' His voice dipped. 'You're a clever woman. Surely you've got *some* idea.'

He saw her touch her tongue to her mouth. Heard the sigh which escaped from her lips and a heavy beat of satisfaction squeezed his heart as he met her hungry gaze. He reached out and pulled her into his arms and instantly she melted against him, the quick tilt of her face silently urging him to kiss her.

So he did.

He kissed her for a long time—long enough for her to start wriggling distractedly, in a way which only stoked his growing desire. He covered her lips in kisses, then turned his mouth to her throat, loving the way her head fell back to give him access to her neck and revelling in the way her thick hair brushed so sensually against his hand. He undid the robe and bent his head to kiss her tiny breasts, flicking his tongue hungrily over her thrusting nipples. And when her hips circled in wordless plea against his aching groin, he inched his fingers up her thigh. Up over the silken surface of her skin he stroked her until at last he found her tight little nub and began to play with her and she was begging him not to stop. Until she was letting him back her up against the dining-room table and he was seriously thinking about sweeping all the crystal and silver and breakfast remains to the floor—and to hell with the mess—when he drew back and looked down into her dazed face.

'Let's go to bed,' he growled, his hands on her shoulders now.

Tara's throat constricted. Her breasts were aching and the syrupy heat between her thighs was making her wish he'd start touching her there again. She wished he hadn't stopped. That he'd just carried on with what he'd been doing and ravished her right there, in the dining room. She might have only had sex once before, but she badly wanted to do it again. She wanted to be carried along on an unstoppable tide of passion like the first time—she didn't want to have to make a *decision* about her actions.

But that was naïve—and short-sighted. She couldn't regard sex like candy—something she could just take when she felt like it. Not when there were so many issues they still hadn't addressed. Wouldn't that be totally irresponsible? There were a baby and a future to think of.

And without that baby she wouldn't be here in his arms like this, would she? She would be back home in Ireland while Lucas carried on with the rest of his life without her.

'No,' she said, shrugging his hands from her shoulders and taking a step backwards, even though her quivering skin still seemed to bear the delicious imprint of his fingers. With firm fingers she pulled the front of her robe together and knotted the belt tightly. 'This is not going to happen.'

His expression told her he didn't believe her. To be honest, she couldn't quite believe it herself.

'Are you serious?' he demanded.

'That's the whole point, Lucas,' she said, and suddenly her voice acquired a note of urgency as she stared into his beautiful face. 'I am. Very serious. I mean, what precisely are you offering me here?'

The flattening of his mouth told its own story. A cynical indication that he now found himself on familiar territory—that these were female demands being thrown at him, something which had been happening all his life. 'I should have thought it was perfectly obvious what I'm offering you, Tara,' he said. 'Sex, pure and simple. Because the bottom line is that we still want each another—surely you're not going to deny that?'

No. She couldn't deny what was obviously the truth—not when her nipples were pushing insistently against her robe, and his frustrated gaze indicated that their silent plea hadn't gone unnoticed.

'So why not capitalise on that?' he continued, with silky assurance. 'Stay with me here in New York and be my lover?'

The passing seconds seemed to drag into minutes as his words sank in. 'Your lover?' she verified slowly, thinking it was an inaccurate description when there was no actual *love* involved.

'Sure. It makes perfect sense. I can make sure you look after yourself and we can enjoy some pretty incredible downtime.' He gave a slow smile as his gaze travelled to the tiny pulse which was hammering at her neck. 'What's not to like?'

The fact he had to ask was telling, but Tara reminded herself that Lucas had never been known for his sensitivity to other people's feelings. She told herself he wasn't trying to insult her, or hurt her—he was just doing what he always did and taking what he wanted. And right now he wanted sex.

Perhaps if she'd been a different kind of woman she might have agreed. If she'd been worldly-wise she might have smiled contentedly and sealed the deal in the master bedroom of this luxury hotel suite. But not only was she inexperienced, she was also afraid. Afraid she would read more into physical intimacy than Lucas ever intended. Afraid of falling under his spell as she'd seen so many other women do and then being heartbroken when he tired of her, as inevitably he would. After all, this passion had happened so suddenly—it was likely to end just as abruptly, even if he hadn't already had a track record for short-lived affairs.

She still knew so little about him. He was the father of her child yet she didn't have a clue what his own childhood had been like, because he'd never told her. Just as he hadn't told her what—if any—role he wanted to play in their baby's life. Wasn't the sensible thing to do to stay here and address all these issues in a calm and collected way? Not let desire warp her judgement and threaten to turn her into an emotional wreck.

'Yes, I will stay here,' she said slowly and

then, before he could touch her again and make her resolve waver, she started backing towards the door. 'But not as your lover, although I will continue to be your housekeeper.'

'My...housekeeper?' he repeated blankly.

'Why not? That was the role you originally offered me, before—'

'Before you spent the night in my bed?' he growled.

'It wasn't the whole night, Lucas. I left shortly after two a.m., if you remember.' She cleared her throat and forged on. 'If you're moving into an apartment you'll need someone in post here and nobody knows the job better than me. It'll allow us to get to know one another better and to think about what's best for the future.'

'Wow,' he said sarcastically. 'That sounds like fun.'

She told herself afterwards that he could have tried to persuade her otherwise, but he didn't. Of course he didn't. Maybe he was already having second thoughts. As he stood silhouetted against the Manhattan skyline, he seemed to symbolise cool, dark composure—while she felt churned-up, misplaced and frustrated.

'I'd just like us to be honest with each other. You know. Open and transparent. Surely that's not too much to ask?' But her voice was a dying croak and her cheeks burning hot, as she turned away from his mocking gaze and fled from the dining room.

CHAPTER EIGHT

'Tara.' Lucas sucked in an impatient breath. 'What the *hell* do you think you're doing?'

A bright clump of hair was falling untidily into her eyes as the apartment door swung open and Tara stepped inside, dumping two bulging bags of groceries on the floor right by his feet.

'I'm bringing home the shopping,' she answered. 'What does it look like I'm doing?'

With a snort of something which felt like rage, Lucas picked up the bags and carried them into the kitchen, aware that she was following him and that his temper was building in a way which was becoming annoying familiar. He waited until he had planted the hessian sacks in the centre of the large table before turning round to confront her. She could be so stubborn! So infuriatingly hard-working! Maybe it had been a mistake to move out of the luxury hotel and into a place of his own, so that Tara could resume her housekeeper duties—especially if she was going to keep up this kind of pace. But she had insisted, hadn't she? Had set her lips in a firm and determined line, and Lucas had found himself going along with her wishes.

'You shouldn't be carrying heavy weights,' he objected.

'Two bags of shopping is hardly what I'd call heavy. Women in rural Ireland have been shifting far more than that for centuries.'

'But we aren't *in* rural Ireland!' he exploded. 'We're in the centre of Manhattan and there are plenty of services which will have stuff delivered right to your door. So why don't you use one of them?'

'What, and never go outside to see the day?' she retorted. 'Cooped up on the seventy-seventh floor of some high-rise apartment block so that I might as well be living on Mars?'

'This happens to be one of the best addresses in all of New York City!' he defended, through gritted teeth.

'I'm not disputing that, Lucas, and I'm not denying that it's very nice—but if I'm not careful I'll never get to see anyone and that's not how I like to live. I've discovered an old-fashioned Italian supermarket which isn't too many blocks away. And I like going there—I've become very friendly with the owner's wife and she's offered to teach me how to make real pasta.'

Remembering the Polish restaurant she'd taken him to in Dublin what now seemed like light years ago, Lucas silently counted to ten as Tara began putting away the groceries.

'At least you seem to be settling in okay,' he observed, watching her sweater ride up to show a narrow white strip of skin as she reached up to put some coffee beans in the cupboard.

'Indeed I am, though it's certainly very different from life in Ballykenna. Or Dublin, for that matter. But it's not so bad.' She pushed tubs of olives and fresh juice into the refrigerator and bent to pick up a speck of something from the granite floor. 'And the people are the same as people everywhere.'

There was a pause as he watched her tuck an errant wave of hair behind her ear, which somehow seemed only to emphasise its habitual untidiness.

'You know, you're really going to have to do something about your appearance,' he said.

Her shoulders stiffened and, when she turned round, her amber eyes were hooded. 'Why?' she demanded suspiciously. 'What's wrong with it?'

He made a dismissive movement towards her outfit—a gesture provoked by frustration as well as disbelief that his life had been so comprehensively turned upside down by one annoyingly stubborn woman. He still couldn't get his head round the fact that she was pregnant, and not just because it was such an alien concept to a man who had never wanted a child of his own. It was compounded by the fact that she didn't look pregnant yet—and her body was as slim as it had ever been. Not that he'd seen any of it, he thought moodily. Not since that first morning, when they'd very nearly had sex on the dining-room table, before she'd had second thoughts and pushed him away.

What woman had ever refused him?

None, he thought grimly. Tara Fitzpatrick was the first.

The painful jerk at his groin punished him for the erotic nature of his thoughts, yet for once he seemed powerless to halt them. They'd been living in close proximity for almost three weeks yet not once had she wavered in her determination to keep their relationship platonic. He shook his head.

Not once.

At first, he'd thought her stand-off might be motivated by pride, or a resolve to get some kind of commitment from him before agreeing to have sex again, despite her defiant words about not wanting marriage. He'd thought the undoubted sizzle of chemistry which erupted whenever they were together would be powerful enough to wear down her defences. To make her think: what the hell? And then give into what they both wanted.

But she hadn't. And hadn't he felt a grudging kind of respect for her resilience, even if it was making him ache so badly every night?

Perhaps it was that frustration which had made him go out and find this apartment. Tara had been complaining that with fleets of chambermaids and receptionists and waiters, there was nothing much for her to do at the hotel—so he had ordered Brandy to come up with some more rental places for him to look at. Eventually she had found a penthouse condominium on West Fifty-Third Street, a place which had caused even his jaded palate to flicker with interest as Brandy had shown him and Tara through each large and echoing room. Eight hundred feet above the ground, the vast condo had oversized windows which commanded amazing views over park, river, city and skyline. There was a library, a wine room, a well-equipped gym in the basement and a huge pool surrounded by a vertical garden. Most women would have been blown away by the undeniable opulence and upmarket address.

But Tara wasn't like most women, he was rapidly coming to realise. She had been uncharacteristically quiet when he'd given her an initial tour of the building. He'd watched her suspiciously eying Brandy and she had then proceeded to exclaim that he couldn't possibly be planning to live in a place that size. He remembered the shock on Brandy's face—probably worried she was about to lose her commission. But that was exactly what he was planning to do, he had explained. In New York you needed to display the trappings of success in order to be taken seriously, and luxury was the best way in which to go about it.

'Wealth inspires confidence,' he'd told her sternly afterwards, but she had shrugged as if she didn't care and he thought she probably didn't.

'You still haven't told me what's wrong with my appearance!' Her soft Irish brogue voice broke into his thoughts as she closed the door of the refrigerator and, plucking her navy-blue overall from a hook on the back of the door, began to shrug it on.

He stared at her. Where did he begin? Aware of the volatility of her mood—something he guessed had to do with fluctuating hormones—Lucas strove to find the right words. 'In Ireland you used to cook dinner whenever I had people over, and I'd like to be able to entertain here, too. In fact, I've arranged to hold a small dinner next week.' He jerked his head towards the impressive vista of skyscrapers. 'Show off the view.'

'It sounds as if there's a "but" coming,' she observed as she did up the last button of her uniform.

Lucas sighed. Maybe there was no easy way to say this. 'That…that thing you insist on wearing,' he said, his gaze sweeping over the offending item and noticing for the first time that her breasts seemed a little bigger than before and that the material was straining very slightly across the bust. A pulse hammered at his temple. 'It's not really very suitable for serving guests.'

'But you never complained when I wore it in Dublin!'

'In Dublin, you came over as someone mildly eccentric—while here you're in danger of being classified as some kind of screwball.'

'Some kind of screwball,' she repeated, in a hollow voice. 'Is that what you think?'

He wasn't surprised to see her face whiten but he was surprised how uncomfortable it made him feel. 'No, it's not what *I* think and it wasn't meant to be an insult, Tara,' he amended hastily. 'Anyway, there's a simple solution.'

'Oh, really?' she said moodily.

'Sure. You can go shopping. Get yourself some new clothes. It's fixable. I'm happy to pay for whatever it takes.'

He thought that a man might reasonably expect to see a woman's eyes light up at the prospect of a lavish buying expedition when someone else was paying. But Tara failed to oblige. He could see her biting her lip and for one awful moment he thought she was going to cry and that made him feel oddly uncomfortable. Her face screwed itself up into a fierce expression but when she spoke, her voice was quite steady.

'Whatever it takes,' she repeated. 'You're saying you want me to buy new clothes to make sure that I look the part—whatever the part is?'

'That's one way of looking at it.' He flicked her unruly curls a glance. 'And maybe you could do something about your hair while you're at it.'

She drew herself up very straight. 'So what you're really saying is that you want to make me look nothing like myself?'

'That's a rather dramatic summary of what I just said, Tara. Think of it as making the best of yourself for once.'

'You certainly seem to have been giving it some thought.' Suddenly that fierce look was back. 'Yet you didn't even bother asking me what the doctor said when I went to see him yesterday, did you, Lucas?'

Lucas met the accusation in her eyes, his body growing tense. He knew he was still in denial about impending fatherhood. That he was doing what he always did when confronted with something he didn't want to deal with, or which caused him pain. He blocked it. Locked it away. Stored it in a dark place never to be examined again. But you couldn't keep doing that when there was a baby involved. No matter how much he tried to pretend it wasn't happening. He kept thinking that one morning he was going to open his eyes and discover that he was the same Lucas as before, one with no ties or commitments.

And that was never going to happen.

And lately he'd been experiencing the occasional flicker of curiosity—uneasy little splinters of thought which spiked away at him at the dead of night when he lay in bed, aching for Tara. He kept remembering the final line of the letter written by the woman who had subjected him to a life of misery. His mother. Except that she was *not* his real mother, despite the fact that she had spent her life pretending to be. Surely no real mother would have treated their child with such disregard and cruelty. And surely no real mother would have tried to justify their behaviour with the flimsiest of excuses. His mouth hardened with contempt. She had done it because she was desperate for the love of a man who didn't really want her. Because she had put her desire for Diego Gonzalez above everything else, hopelessly pursuing it with single-minded determination which had pushed her adopted son into the shadows. And that was what people did for *love*, he summarised bitterly as he processed the accusation Tara had just thrown at him. They manipulated and they lied.

'Okay. Tell me. What *did* the doctor say?' he said.

But his dutiful question seemed to irritate her more than please her and she answered it like someone recounting the words by rote. She and the baby had been pronounced perfectly healthy, she told him tartly, and she had been booked in for a scan the following week. Her eyes had narrowed like a watchful cat. 'Perhaps you'd like to accompany me, Lucas?'

'We'll see,' he said, non-committally, pulling back the cuff of his shirt to glance at his watch. 'I have a meeting scheduled, so I'd better run. And in the meantime, do you want to organise yourself a shopping trip?'

Tara met the faintly impatient question in his eyes and tried to tell herself he wasn't being unreasonable, though in her heart she wasn't sure she believed it. But then, she was mixed up and confused and out of her depth in so many ways. Frightened about the future and unsure about the present. Every morning she awoke to a slew of different emotions but she'd refused to let them show, knowing that bravado was the only way of surviving this bizarre situation.

Her feelings about Lucas didn't help and she thought how much easier it would be if she didn't want him so badly. If only she could blind herself to the certainty that he could break her heart. She sighed, because in many ways she couldn't fault him. He had accepted her demand for no intimacy with composure and then hadn't she driven herself half mad wishing he hadn't accepted it *quite* so calmly? Perhaps she'd imagined he would come banging on her door at night, demanding she let him in. Or just walk in without asking, slide in between her sheets and take her into his arms. And wasn't there a big part of her that wished he *would* adopt such a masterful role and take the decision right out of her hands?

But no. He'd found this apartment within walking distance of Central Park—with the assistance of the intimidating Brandy—and had booked her in to see a wonderful obstetrician in Lexington, who had immediately made her feel at ease. In some ways their familiar working pattern had simply been transferred to a brand-new setting, except that here she had no bicycle because even she had to concede that in New York it was too dangerous.

Yet despite their superficial compatibility, she recognised that he was still a stranger to her. Despite that one-off night of intimacy, she knew no more about Lucas Conway than when they'd been living in Dublin. Back then it hadn't been relevant—but now she was carrying his baby and it was. Didn't she have the *right* to know something about him?

'If I agree to smarten up my appearance to fit in with your billionaire image...' she hesitated, lifting her gaze to his '...will you agree to do something for me?'

His green gaze was shot with cynicism. 'Ah. This sounds like bargaining territory to me.'

'Maybe it is—but that's irrelevant. Because I know nothing about you. Do you realise that, Lucas? You're the father of my baby and yet you're practically a stranger to me...' As her words tailed off she heard a trace of vulnerability in her own voice. Did he hear it too? Was that why his face darkened? But he relented, didn't he? Even if he did clip out the words like bullets.

'What do you want to know?'

Everything. But Tara sensed that if she

asked for too much, she would get nothing at all.

'What was in that letter?' she questioned suddenly.

'The letter?' he said, and she knew he was playing for time.

'You know very well which letter. The one you received just before you came out here.'

The one which made you act so strangely and look so haunted.

She hesitated and said it exactly as it was. 'Which made you look so angry. Who was it from, Lucas?'

It was then that Lucas realised just how much Tara Fitzpatrick *did* know about him. Probably more than any other living person. His mouth hardened. But that was the thing about having a housekeeper. You thought they just existed in the shadows of your life. You thought they were there simply to enable things to run smoothly—but in reality they were watching you and listening to you. Absorbing all the comings and goings like a detached observer. And although her pregnancy meant Tara could no longer be described as detached—didn't that make her entitled to know the truth?

A truth he had firmly locked away. A truth he had never talked about with anyone before.

His throat dried as he looked into the soft question in her eyes and suddenly he found himself wanting to confide in her—to share the ugly facts with someone. 'It was from my father's…' His mouth twisted as he said the word. 'His attorney.

'Your *father*?' She blinked at him in surprise.

He nodded. 'He died a few months back.'

'You never said—'

'Well, I'm saying now. There was no reason to tell you before,' he said. 'And before you look at me with that reproachful gaze—I didn't go to his funeral because I hated him and he hated me.' He paused for a moment, long enough to get his breathing under control but he could do nothing about the painful clench of his heart. 'They found a letter from my mother among his belongings. A letter addressed to me, which I never received, even though it was written a long time ago, just before she died. But it seemed she didn't have the sense or the wherewithal to give it to her own lawyer. She entrusted it to her husband, which was a dumb thing to do because he kept it all this time and I only got to hear about it after his death.'

Her face creased with concentration as if she was trying to piece together a puzzle of facts. 'So is New York where you were born?'

He shook his head, his laugh bitter as, unwittingly, she asked the most pertinent question of all. 'It's where I grew up. I don't know where I was born because last week I discovered that my mother and father weren't my real parents.'

'You mean…' she frowned again '…that they kept that fact hidden from you?'

'Yes, they did. Though there's a more accurate way of putting it. They lied to me, Tara. All through my life they lied.' He saw her wince. 'Because they couldn't bear to tell me the truth.'

'And was the truth so very awful?' she whispered.

'Judge for yourself.' There was silence for a moment before he shrugged, but his shoulders still felt as if they were carrying a heavy weight. 'The woman I called my mother was in her forties when she married a man who was decades younger. She was a hugely wealthy heiress and he was a poor, good-looking boy from Argentina—who happened to have a pretty big gambling habit. Her Alabama family cut her off when she married Diego and the two of them moved to Manhattan. In her letter she explained that he wanted a child but her age meant she was unable to give him one.' He gave a bitter laugh. 'So she did what she'd spent her whole life doing. She tried to solve a problem by buying her way out of it. That's when she bought me.' He gave a bitter laugh. 'My mother bought me, Tara. But when the deal was done she discovered that having me around wasn't the quick solution to her troubles she thought I would be. She'd bought me, but she didn't want me and neither did Diego. Suddenly I was in the way and a child isn't as easy to dispose of as one of the fancy sports cars my father loved to drive.'

And Tara stared at him dumbly, in horror and in shock.

CHAPTER NINE

'YOUR MOTHER *BOUGHT* YOU?' Tara demanded, eventually getting her voice back. 'She actually paid money for you?'

'She did.' His jaw tightened. 'I guess the illegal trade in selling babies has always gone on and back then it was pretty unregulated. She found someone who was willing to part with their infant child—for the right price, of course.'

'I can't believe it,' she breathed.

But Lucas seemed to barely hear her. It was as if having bottled it up—that he could do nothing to now stop the words spilling bitterly from his mouth.

'A child's memory only kicks in fragmentally,' he continued harshly. 'But I gradually became aware of the fact that he seemed to resent me from the get-go and then to hate me—only I could never understand why. It couldn't have helped that he obviously felt trapped in a marriage to a woman he clearly didn't love—only he loved her fortune too much to ever walk away.' But that hadn't lessened the tension, had it? His mother sobbing and kneeling on the floor in front of her younger husband, begging him not to leave her. And Diego gloating like a boastful schoolboy about the lipstick she'd found on his collar. Lucas snapped out of his painful reverie to find Tara staring at him, her eyes like two amber jewels in her pale face.

'What…happened?' she whispered.

He shrugged. 'They sent me away to boarding school in Europe to get me out of the way. And when I came home for the holidays…' he paused and maybe admitting this was the hardest part of all, harder even than the sharp blows to his kidneys '…he used to beat me up,' he finished, on a rush.

'But, surely he couldn't get away with something like that?'

'Oh, he was very careful. And clever, too. He only used to mark me where it wouldn't show.' He heard her sharp intake of breath and she opened her lips as if to say something, but he carried on—wanting to excise the dark poison which had lived inside him for so long. 'The summer I realised I could hurt him back was the last summer I ever came here and that's when I broke all ties with them.'

'But what about your mother?' she breathed. 'Do you think she was aware that Diego was cruel to you?'

He gave a cynical laugh as he gazed at her with weary eyes. 'Do you really think it's possible for a woman not to know when a child is being beaten within the home, even in a house as big and cold and dysfunctional as ours?'

'Oh, Lucas.' Her bottom lip had grown pinker from where she'd been worrying it with her teeth and he saw the genuine consternation on her face. 'That's terrible. I can't—'

'I didn't tell you because I wanted your sympathy, Tara.' Ruthlessly, he cut across her faltered words. 'I told you because you asked and because you of all people now have a right to know. Maybe now you can understand why I started a new life for myself and left the old one far behind. When my mother died my father was such a gambler it wasn't long before there was no money left to pay for my schooling in Switzerland, so at sixteen I got myself a job as a bellhop in a fancy Swiss hotel—'

'So that bit was true,' she interrupted wonderingly before offering an explanation to the frowning question in his eyes. 'There were rumours swirling around Dublin that you'd been a bellhop but I couldn't ever imagine you doing a job like that.'

For the first time, he smiled—and the rare flash of humour on his troubled face made Tara's heart turn over with an emotion she didn't dare analyse.

'You'd be surprised at what a comprehensive education it was,' he said. 'I watched and learned from all the customers who'd made money and a couple of them gave me advice on how to make it big. When I got to Ireland I changed my name and that changed everything. I worked hard and saved even harder and I had a little luck sprinkled over me on the way.' He gave a short laugh. 'Though maybe I deserved a little luck by then.'

But Tara didn't seem interested in the details about how he'd made his fortune. Instead she was frowning with intensity, as she did when she was trying to work something out, often a new recipe.

'I guess you did.' She hesitated. 'But going back to the letter.'

'I thought we'd moved on from the letter.'

Seemingly undaunted, she continued. 'Was there any information about your birth mother in it?'

'I know her name.'

'And have you…have you followed it up?'

'What do you think?' he snapped.

'Don't you think you might? I mean, you might have…' She shrugged. 'Well, you might have other relatives who—'

'I'm not interested in relatives,' he said coldly. 'I've had it with family. Surely you can understand why? And I don't want to talk about it any more.'

He stared at her almost resentfully, wanting to blame her for having unburdened himself like this, but the hard stir of his groin was making him think about something other than the past. The flood of desire was a welcome antidote to the pain which had resulted from his confession and had left him feeling as if someone had blasted him with an emotional blowtorch. And now he was empty and hurting inside. Did she sense that? Could she detect the hunger in his body which was demanding release? Was that why she walked over to where he was standing and wordlessly hooked her arms around his neck, pressing her face against his cheek and planting there a kiss so soft that it made his heart turn over with something nameless and unfamiliar? Something underpinned with danger, despite all its dark deliciousness.

He wanted to push her away and compose himself but his need for her was stronger than his need for equilibrium and he pulled her into his arms and held her close. His heart pounded. So close. The faint scent of her sex was already redolent in the air and something inside him melted as instantly as ice hitting hot water. Their gazes clashed for the nanosecond it took before their lips fused and they shared the most passionate kiss he could ever remember. And when there was no breath left in his lungs, he reluctantly drew his head away, his eyes silently asking her a question and she answered it with a silent nod. This time she didn't call a halt to what was happening as he laced his fingers in hers. Instead, she let him lead her to the master bedroom, where he pulled the navy-blue ribbon from her hair and all those unruly waves tumbled around her shoulders with fiery profusion.

'Lucas?' she said, and he heard the uncertainty in her voice—as if wanting him to define what was happening. But he couldn't. Or rather, he wouldn't. He would never lie about his feelings for her. This didn't go deep. It was one level only. Simple physical need. 'I want you,' he said, very deliberately. 'That's all.'

Tara sucked in a ragged breath, wondering if it could be enough. But it had to be enough, because nothing else was on offer. And surely she could be grown up enough to admit that she wanted him—unconditionally. Surely she wasn't demanding words of love or commitment in order to enjoy sex with the father of her baby. Her mouth dried. Some people might say they'd already made progress in their relationship because he'd confided in her—something which had never happened before. He'd told her the awful truth about his upbringing—which made even her own seem less bad. Should she have filled him in on some of her own, awful personal history? She thought not. Not then and certainly not now when he seemed to need her very badly, and all she wanted was to bring a little comfort and joy into his life. Hers, too. Was that so wrong?

'I want you, too,' she said shakily.

'But before we go any further, there's one thing we need to get straight, which is that I'm not offering undying love, or certain commitment. I can't put my hand on my heart and promise to be with you for the rest of my life, Tara,' he emphasised harshly. 'Because that's not what I do. You know that.'

She shook her head. 'I don't care.'

She could see his throat constrict as he undid the buttons of her uniform before quickly dispensing with the T-shirt and jeans beneath. And when he began to tug impatiently at his silk shirt, she found herself fantasising about what their baby might look like when it was born. Would it be a boy? she wondered yearningly as he lifted her up and laid her down on the bed. A boy who would grow up to be like his father—charismatic and powerful but with a dark side which was hiding so much pain? Or would it be a red-headed little girl, destined to be swamped by her own insecurities?

But her questions were forgotten as his naked body was revealed to her—all honed muscle and soft shadow and the subtle gleam of olive skin. His limbs were hair-roughened and his desire was achingly obvious and she should have been daunted but she wasn't. She stared at him with longing as the bed dipped beneath his weight and when he took her in his arms again, his skin felt deliciously warm against hers. Was it the conversation they'd just had which suddenly made Tara feel less of a conquest and more of an equal? Which gave her the courage to explore his body in a way she would never have dared do before? Tentatively at first but with growing assurance, she stroked his skin, her fingertips running over washboard abs, down over the flat hardness of his stomach, to whisper shyly at the dark brush of hair beyond.

'Tara?' he said softly.

'What?'

'Don't keep doing that.'

'You don't like it?'

'I like it too much,' he growled.

'What…what shall I do instead?'

He gave a soft laugh. 'Part your thighs for me.'

She lifted her head as she did exactly that, their gazes clashing as, very deliberately, he slipped his hand between her legs and began to finger the creamy-moist folds with a light touch which sent a wild shudder through her body.

'L-Lucas,' she breathed.

'Shh… Don't say a word. Just feel it. Feel what I'm doing to you. It's good, isn't it?'

'Y-yes. It's very good.'

With delicate precision he strummed her where she was wet and aching, until she was writhing helplessly on the mattress and making unintelligible little gasps. Sensation speared at her with each feather-light touch as he propelled her towards some starry summit, so that she felt like an unexploded firework which was hurtling though the sky. And when the eruption came, he entered her at the same moment—so she could feel herself still clenching around his hardness as their bodies were intimately joined. It felt exquisitely erotic and unexpectedly emotional and as she looked up into the dark mask of his beautiful face, she touched her fingertips to his cheek.

'Lucas,' she said shakily, trying to bite back the soft words of affection which were hovering on her lips.

He stilled as he searched her face. 'It doesn't hurt?'

'No. It's…it's gorgeous.'

'I've never done it without protection before,' he husked. 'Never.'

She couldn't respond to his appreciative

murmur because her eager body was short-circuiting her addled brain, making rational thought impossible as a second orgasm swept her up on a breathless wave. In fact there was no time to address his question until afterwards, when he had choked out his own pleasure and she could feel the sticky trickle of his seed running down her thigh in a way which felt deliciously intimate. Her heart was pounding and her skin was suffused with satisfied heat, but she forced herself to turn over to face the Manhattan skyline outside the window as she tried to get her muddled thoughts into some kind of order.

Because she could sense she was on the brink of something risky. Something which needed to be reined in and controlled. Yes, they'd just had the most amazing sex but in the middle of it hadn't Lucas gloated about never having had unprotected sex before while she'd been getting all emotional about him? And that was the fundamental difference between them. He required sex and nothing more and so she needed to be vigilant about her emotions. To make sure she didn't get sucked into a bubble of love and longing which would burst at the slightest provocation.

'Tara,' he said softly.

His finger was tracing a delicate path between her buttocks and she felt herself quiver in response. 'What?' she questioned, as casually as possible.

'I suspect what we've just done has made you change your mind about us being lovers.'

His assurance was as unshakable as his arrogance and she wanted to tell him that, no, she hadn't changed her mind at all. She wanted to declare that this had been another impetuous mistake which mustn't be repeated. But she couldn't keep running away from the consequences of her actions, could she? She couldn't keep letting sex 'happen' and then act like a scared little girl afterwards.

What she wanted was impossible. Like most people she wanted what she'd never had—in her case a secure home and a child raised within a loving family—despite all her proud protestations to the contrary. Lucas had offered none of these things and, having heard about his own childhood, she could understand why. It didn't matter that his parents hadn't been his birth parents—what mattered was that they had lied and been cruel to him. His whole upbringing had been built on a web of deceit and had destroyed his trust in other people. No wonder he was such a commitment-phobe who had never wanted marriage. No wonder he sometimes seemed to view women as the enemy, because to him they were. His birth mother had sold him and his adopted mother had lied to him and condoned her husband's violence towards him.

But he'd offered to support her and the baby, hadn't he? He hadn't said he wanted to be hands-on, but surely that was a start— a single block on which to build. She didn't know what the future held—nobody did—but there was no reason why they couldn't have a grown-up relationship within certain boundaries. Just so long as she didn't start weaving unattainable fantasises—and maybe for that reason alone, she needed to maintain an element of independence.

So she turned over and touched her fingertip to his face, tracing it slowly along the outline of his sensual lips. 'Yes, I'll be your lover,' she said. 'But I'm not going to give up my role as housekeeper.'

His eyes narrowed. 'Are you out of your mind?'

'Not at all. I need to work and that's my job. Otherwise, what am I going to do all day while you wheel and deal—go out to lunch and have my nails painted?' Her smile was serene as she met his disbelieving expression and she wouldn't have been human if she hadn't enjoyed that small moment of triumph. 'I've never had any desire to be a kept woman, Lucas, and I don't intend to start now.'

CHAPTER TEN

SUNLIGHT CAME STREAMING in through the huge windows, bathing Tara's body with a delicious glow, though the only thing she was really aware of was Lucas's hand, which was splayed proprietorially over one breast, while the other was tucked possessively around her waist. But possessive was a misnomer and any sense she *belonged* to him was simply an illusion, she reminded herself fiercely. The touchy-feely-couldn't-seem-to-keep-his-hands-off-her side of his character was just another feature of the fantastic sex they'd recently enjoyed. A physical reaction, that was all.

He was lazily stroking her nipple so that it was proud and aching, even though she had just gasped out one of the shuddering orgasms which had become so much a part of her daily life. Yet the crazy thing was that the man beside her felt as much of a stranger as he'd ever done—despite having told her about his childhood and despite having just been deep inside her body. Had she hoped that physical intimacy would automatically morph into mental intimacy? That the bond between them would grow stronger—maybe even unbreakable—the longer they spent together wrapped in each other's arms like this?

Yes, she had. Guilty on all counts. But what did she know about such matters when he was her first and only lover? Her mentor, too. In the most delicious way possible, he had tutored her in every aspect of sex. He'd taught her how to uninhibitedly enjoy her body and not to be shy about expressing her needs, but none of that seemed to have impacted on their relationship. Despite the physical closeness of sharing their bed each night and the often teasing banter they enjoyed much as before, nothing fundamental had changed within their relationship. Emotionally, at least, he was as detached as he had ever been.

Was that because, in spite of his obvious disapproval, she'd insisted in maintaining her role as his housekeeper—thus reinforcing the boss/employee dynamic which had always existed between them? She didn't think so. What else was she going to do all day if she wasn't cooking and cleaning—lie around in some cliché of a negligee waiting for Lucas to return from one of his business meetings? She would go out of her mind with boredom if she did that. Anyway, she didn't have a negligee—clichéd or otherwise—because somehow she still hadn't got around to the shopping trip Lucas had suggested she take to avoid looking like 'a screwball'.

'Are you awake?' His murmured voice was soft against her hair.

Her thoughts still full of fundamental insecurities, Tara nodded. 'Mmm…'

The bedclothes rustled as he shifted, turning her round to face him so that their eyes were level and Tara prayed her face didn't give away her feelings. Feelings she was trying desperately hard to hide, because she knew Lucas was no stranger to the emotion she and countless women before her had experienced…

She was falling for him. Falling deep and falling hard.

She was scared to use the word *love* but it was the only one which seemed appropriate to describe the see-sawing of her feelings and the great rush of joy which powered her heart whenever he walked into the room. When he kissed her she sometimes felt she could faint with pleasure and when he made love to her, her happiness threatened to spill over. It didn't seem to matter how much she tried to deny what she was feeling, it made no difference. She wasn't sure how it had happened. If it was because he'd taken her innocence and made her pregnant.

Or because, beneath his glossy patina of success, he was wounded and hurting inside and that made her want to reach out to protect him?

He lifted a strand of hair and wound it slowly around his finger and Tara was reminded of one of those fishermen back home—the way they used to slowly reel in their catch, before leaving the floundering fish gasping for air on the quayside.

'You still haven't been shopping,' he observed.

'I know.' She shrugged her bare shoulders. 'But I haven't seemed to be able to find the time.'

'Then *make* the time, Tara. Better still. Why don't I schedule an appointment with a personal shopper and drop you off at Bloomingdale's? That way you won't be able to wriggle out of it the way you seem to have been doing.'

She blinked. 'What's Bloomingdale's?'

He frowned. 'You're kidding?'

'Lucas, this is a big city and I'm exploring it the best I can! I can't be expected to know every single name which trips off your tongue.'

'It just happens to be one of the best department stores in the city, possibly the world,' he commented drily. 'And I'll drop you off there tomorrow morning, on my way to work.'

'But we might not be able to get an appointment so soon,' she objected.

His brief smile managed to be both dismissive and entitled. 'Don't worry about that,' he drawled as he parted her thighs with insistent fingers. 'We'll get one. You haven't forgotten that you're cooking dinner for six on Friday, have you?'

'No, Lucas. I haven't forgotten. I've been racking my brains to come up with a menu for days.' She swallowed. 'And you doing that to me isn't exactly helping me work out what to give them for dessert.'

'Damn the dessert,' he growled.

But by the following morning Tara felt sick with nerves at the thought of presenting herself to a professional stylist, horribly aware of the plainness and age of her bra and pants and wishing she could skip the whole ordeal. Because it turned out that Lucas had been right and there were any number of slots available for a man like him at short notice.

Reluctantly, she joined him in the back of his car, which then proceeded to get snarled up in the early-morning traffic. It was stop-start all the way and Tara started to feel even more queasy. 'It's very stuffy in here.'

'I'll turn up the A/C.'

'I don't want any more air-conditioning. I want to get out and walk,' she croaked.

He shot her a quick glance. 'Are you okay?'

'I will be when I'm outside in the fresh air.'

'Fine. Come on, I'll walk you there.'

'Honestly, there's no need. I can find the store perfectly well on my own and I don't want you to be late for your meeting.'

'Tara,' he said patiently, his voice underpinned with a hint of impatience. 'It's pointless objecting. I'm taking you there. End of discussion.'

He tapped the glass and spoke to his driver, then helped Tara out of the car. She saw a glamorous woman blinking at her in bemusement as she stepped onto the sidewalk in her sweatpants and trainers, swamped by a big old anorak she'd brought with her from Dublin. But it was great to be outside, despite the stationary traffic and ever-hooting cars. As Lucas fell into a steady walk beside her, she thought how well he seemed to know the streets and when she remarked on this, he shrugged.

'I grew up near here.'

'Whereabouts?'

'It doesn't matter.'

'I think it does.' She came to a sudden halt and a speed-walking man who was holding a cup of coffee above his head had to swerve to avoid her. 'I'd like to see where you lived, please.'

Lucas bit back an exasperated retort, but he altered his steps accordingly, making no attempt to hide his displeasure. If it had been any other woman than Tara he would have refused point-blank. He would have delivered a rebuke which suggested that unless she started behaving as he wanted her to behave, their relationship would be over. But it wasn't any other woman. It was Tara and she was pregnant and therefore he could never completely finish a relationship with her because, one way or another, they would be tied through their child for the rest of their lives. He wondered if she had any idea how much that terrified him or if she'd begun to guess at the self-doubts which flooded through him. Was that why there had been a subtle shift in her mood lately? Why she'd become unpredictable and emotional. Had it just dawned on her that he could never be the man she probably wanted him to be? Why, only yesterday when he'd arrived home, her eyes had been red-rimmed from crying and she'd been unwilling to provide an explanation of what had upset her. It was only later that she'd blurted out about hearing a radio request show playing 'Danny Boy', after which she'd been overcome by a wave of temporary homesickness.

Deep down, he knew their situation was untenable in its current form. That in just over six months' time she would give birth to his child and everything would change. He realised that she wanted reassurance he would be there for her, and in the important ways he would. Providing for her financially was always going to be simple—but giving her the emotional support he suspected she needed was not. Why promise to be the man he could never be? Why bolster her hopes, only to smash them and let her down? Surely it would be kinder to let her know where she stood right from the start.

His footsteps slowed as he reached Upper East Side, his heart clenching as he came to a halt outside an opulent mansion which was edged by elegant railings and neatly trimmed greenery. Outwardly, it seemed that very little had changed. There were still those two old-fashioned-looking streetlights he'd used to stare down on from within the echoing lone-liness of his childhood bedroom.

'This is it,' he said reluctantly, his gaze lift-ing upwards to the four-storeyed building.

'Gosh,' breathed Tara, loosening her long scarf as she craned her neck to look up at it. 'It's massive. You must have rattled around in it like peas inside a tin can.'

He gave a bitter smile. 'Oh, I don't know. Furniture and objects can occupy an aston-ishing amount of space and it's amazing what you can do with nineteen rooms and an un-limited budget. Especially when someone else is paying for it.'

'Nineteen rooms?' she verified incredu-lously. 'In New York?'

He nodded. 'The dining room was mod-elled on the one at the Palace of Versailles and there's a hand-painted ballroom with a pure gold ceiling—not to mention a corridor wide enough to ride a bicycle down.'

'Is that what you used to do?'

'Only once,' he said flatly. That had been the first time his 'father' had hit him. His nanny—one in a long line of indifferent women in whose care he'd spent most of his time—had spotted the bruise when he was getting ready for bed, readily accepting his explanation that he'd acquired it after falling over. Later he'd discovered that the nanny in question had been sleeping with Diego. He'd overheard an indiscreet maid exclaiming that the woman had been discovered naked with him on the floor of the library, a litter of used condoms beside them. All he could remember about that particular incident had been his mother screaming. And then sobbing as she had dramatically stabbed at her wrists with a blunt blade which had refused to cut.

Tara stared at him. 'You must have felt very isolated there. My own…' she ventured hesitantly, before plucking up the courage to say it. To reassure him that her own life hadn't been all roses around the cottage door. Well, it had—but there had been very sharp thorns on those roses. 'My own childhood was pretty isolated. In fact, my grandmother—'

'Look, I really don't have time for this,' he said, with an impatient narrowing of his eyes as he glanced at his watch. 'And I have an imminent meeting. The city tour is over and so is the glimpse into my past. Come on, let's get you to Bloomingdale's—it's only ten minutes' walk away.'

His dismissive attitude hurt. It hurt far more than it should have done, but that was a result of her own stubbornness—not something *he* had done. Because Lucas was just behaving in the way he'd always behaved. How many times did he need to say it for her to finally get the message that he wasn't interested in deepening their relationship? He didn't *want* to know about her past. What had made her the person she was. What had made her happy and what had given her pain. She was someone he was forced to spend time with because of the baby and someone he liked having sex with, but that was as far as it went.

So put up or shut up, she told herself fiercely as Bloomingdale's came into view—with all the different flags fluttering in the autumn breeze and a quirkily dressed brunette called

Jessica waiting for them. After initial introductions, she gave Tara a thorough once-over before fixing her with a warm smile and turning to Lucas.

'Don't worry, Mr Conway. She's in good hands.'

Lucas gave a brief nod. 'Thanks. Just do what it takes. I'll be back tomorrow night in time for dinner, Tara. Okay?'

Tara nodded and thought how crazy the whole situation was. Right up until they'd left the apartment that morning they'd been hungrily exploring each other's bodies—yet now, in the cold and clear light of day, she was expected to give him a cool farewell, as if she meant nothing to him.

Because she didn't.

'Right,' said Jessica, turning towards Tara as Lucas's car pulled away from the kerb. 'Let's get this fairy dust working.'

It was an experience Tara had never thought could happen to someone like her. Pushing all her troubled thoughts resolutely from her mind, she felt positively Cinderella-like as Jessica led her through all the plush and beautifully lit departments, which were perfumed with all manner of delicious scents. She'd been planning to purchase only a modest wardrobe but it seemed Lucas had fore-warned the personal shopper this might be the case because she was overruled in pretty much everything.

'I've never owned a shirt like this before,' she observed wonderingly, running her fin-gertips over the delicate fabric. 'I'll save it for best.'

'Ah, but you'll need more than one,' re-sponded Jessica, with a smile. 'Which means you won't have to.'

In the space of a couple of hours, Tara went from being someone who'd never owned a single silk shirt, to someone who now had several. For the snowy New York winter she snuggled into an oversized metal-lic anorak, its hood lined with shaggy faux fur, which Jessica told her was fresh off the runway, while for more formal occasions came a mid-length coat in midnight blue, the warmest coat Tara had ever worn. An ac-companying cobalt scarf was plucked from a rainbow selection and Jessica's gaze trav-elled ruefully to the overly long home-knit, which lay abandoned on a nearby chair like a large and neglected woollen snake. 'You might want to find that another home,' she suggested gently.

Tara felt a momentary pang before being persuaded into the first of many dresses—slinky shirtwaisters and soft knits which Jessica said emphasised her slim frame. Next came boots—long boots and ankle boots—plus a pair of trendy shoes with lace inserts to go with a swingy chiffon shirt and boxy denim jacket. There were exquisite embroidered bras and matching thongs, as well as T-shirt bras with more practical pants. And Tara felt momentarily overwhelmed as she acknowledged that it had been Lucas's murmured appreciation which had made her revel in her own body instead of being ashamed of it. He'd never moaned about the state of her underwear, had he? Not really. He'd always been more concerned in taking it off than complaining about how faded it was.

She blinked away the sudden tears which had sprung to her eyes as she tried on the jeans which were an entirely different breed from the baggy ones which had always been her mainstay. Fashioned from soft and stretchy denim, they hugged her bottom but allowed for future expansion, though there was still no visible sign of a pregnancy bump. She wanted to tell the shopper that in a few months' time none of these gorgeous outfits would fit—but she could hardly start telling her personal business to a complete stranger, could she?

'It's been a pleasure doing business with you, Mrs Conway,' said Jessica as the session drew to a close.

Tara shook her head—despairing at her instinctive pang of yearning at the thought of being Lucas's wife. *It's because your own mother was never married,* she told herself. *Nor her mother before that. You're just secretly craving the respectability you never had, which made your own childhood such a misery. But things are different these days and nobody cares if a child is born out of wedlock.* 'I'm not Lucas's wife,' she said calmly. 'I'm actually his housekeeper—and I was wondering if you happen to sell aprons here?'

To Jessica's credit, she didn't look a bit fazed by what have been an unusual request. 'Of course,' she said. 'Come with me.'

The morning ended with a rock-star experience at the hair salon, where Tara sipped cinnamon-flavoured latte as large chunks were hacked from her curls. The result was…well, unbelievable, really—and several of the stylists had clustered around the mirror to say so. Her hair looked just as thick as before but it was more...manageable somehow. Little fronds framed her face and, where layers had been chopped into it, the colour seemed more intense and the texture more lustrous. She was aware of heads turning as she left the salon in her brand-new jeans, pale jumper and the boxy denim jacket. And she'd never had that experience before. Of men's eyes following her as she slid into the back of the chauffeur-driven car which Lucas had ordered for her.

She remembered her grandmother's disapproval of fancy clothes—understandable given her own monastic upbringing, but a bit tough on a growing teenager who had been forced to wear second-hand outfits, which had only increased the amount of bullying she'd received.

The apartment was quiet and, since Lucas wouldn't be back until tomorrow, she had a whole day and a night without him. The only time she'd been on her own since she'd arrived here—which meant no distractions as she prepared for her very first dinner party in America. She looked down at the list of people he'd invited—an official from the Irish embassy and his wife, an Italian business-man named Salvatore di Luca and his girl-friend Alicia, and an 'unnamed guest' who seemed to have been added since last time she'd looked at it.

She wasn't going to deny that it was going to be weird serving Lucas and his guests and playing the role of servant, all the while knowing she would be sharing his bed once everyone had gone home. But surely it was better that way.

It had to be. Because if they stopped being lovers... She bit her lip and silently corrected herself. *When* they stopped being lovers, if the baby drove a wedge between them, or when he tired of her as history dictated he would—then surely it would be less traumatic not to have become used to being his partner in public, and then have that role wrenched away from her. Such a brutal change of cir-cumstance would surely leave her feeling ne-glected, unloved and unwanted.

And hadn't she already experienced enough of those feelings to last a lifetime?

Smoothing down her pale cashmere sweater, she went into the kitchen, realising that she needed to get a move on with her planning. Without her stack of cookery books, she was forced to fire up her computer to look up some recipes online, but she scrolled through them uninterestedly.

Until suddenly she had a brilliant idea.

CHAPTER ELEVEN

THE FIRST THING Lucas heard when he walked through the door was the sound of music. His steps stilled and he paused to listen, even though he was running late. Irish music. Some softly lilting air which managed to be both mournful and uplifting at the same time—in the way of all Irish music. He frowned as he heard a peel of laughter which sounded familiar and then the chink of crystal, followed by more laughter.

With a quick glance at his watch he moved swiftly towards the library, quietly pushing open the door to see his guests standing with their backs to him, listening to something Tara was saying as she tilted a bottle of champagne into someone's glass.

He almost did a double-take as for a moment he felt as if the light were playing tricks on him, because the woman in question looked like Tara and sounded like Tara, and yet…

He screwed up his eyes.

And *yet*…

Surely that wasn't *Tara*?

Her hair was scooped on top of her head but for once there wasn't a riot of frizzy curls tumbling around her face. The sleek red waves were coiled like sleeping serpents—emphasising the slim, pale column of her neck. He swallowed, because her hair wasn't the only thing which was different. She was wearing a dress. And stockings. And… Again, he frowned. She had on some flirty little apron which made her look… She looked as if she was about to leave for a party where the specified dress code was Sexy French Maid. His groin grew rocky and he realised he didn't want to focus on her appearance, or the evening was going to become one long endurance test before he could take her to bed.

He realised his guests must have heard him for they were turning to greet him and as he apologised for his lateness he saw a wry look on Brett Henderson's face—because, as a world-acclaimed movie star and key member of British acting royalty, he wasn't used to being kept waiting.

But Lucas's somewhat garbled explanations about late planes and fog on the San Franciscan runway were cut short by a dismissive wave from the Irish Embassy official.

'Oh, don't you worry about that, Lucas—we've been fine here.' Seamus Hennessy beamed, and so did his wife, Erin. 'We're hardly missed you at all and Tara's been looking after us grandly, so she has!'

For the first time since he'd walked in, Tara turned to look at him and gave a shy smile, which contrasted with the sensual allure of her outfit, and Lucas was taken aback by the resultant shiver which rippled its way down his spine as he met her heavy-hooded amber gaze. He found himself wishing he could just dismiss the guests, skip supper and take her straight to bed—yet his need for her unsettled him.

'Do you all have drinks?' he questioned pleasantly. 'Good. Tara? I wonder if I could have a quick word in the kitchen.'

He didn't say anything as they left the library and neither did he comment as they passed the dining room, even though he could see she must have gone to a lot of trouble to lay the table for dinner. Unlit candles protruded from centrepiece swathes of fragrant greenery mixed with cherry-coloured roses, and all the crystal and silver was gleaming beneath the diamond shards of the overhead chandelier. He waited until they were in the kitchen and completely out of earshot before he turned on her and the feelings which had been growing inside him now erupted.

'What happened?' he demanded. 'You don't look like you!'

Faint colour stained her cheeks as she glanced down at her outfit before looking up again to meet his accusing gaze. 'You mean you don't like it?'

'I told you to buy yourself some new clothes,' he ground out. 'Not to look like the personification of every man's fantasy maid.'

She screwed up her face. 'It's an apron, Lucas!' she said crossly. 'And perhaps you ought to make your mind up about where you really stand! You were always criticising my old uniform for being too frumpy and now you're complaining that this one is too sexy!'

Confused, he shook his head. 'It's the way you wear it,' he said slowly.

'Or rather, the way you perceive it—which is your problem, not mine. Make up your mind what it is you want because I haven't got the time or the appetite for this. And now, if you'll excuse me—' she lifted her chin in as haughty a gesture as he'd ever seen her use '—I really do need to get on with serving dinner.'

He wanted to reach out and stay her with a hungry kiss but something stopped him and it wasn't just pride. It was anger. And jealousy—and he didn't *do* jealousy or possession.

But the true and very bitter fact seemed to be that he *did*.

He forced himself to snap out of his foul mood and, since he often hosted dinners without a woman by his side, it shouldn't have been a problem. Seamus and Erin were easy company and Salvatore di Luca's latest squeeze worked for the United Nations and had some very illuminating things to say about the current political situation in Europe, which usually would have interested him. But for once he found his attention wandering and the biggest fly in the ointment was Brett Henderson flirting like crazy with Tara. And she wasn't exactly discouraging him, was she? Did she really have to simper like that as she told him how much she'd enjoyed the film in which he'd played a shape-shifting wizard?

Lucas was forced to watch as the mellifluous Englishman returned the love-fest by purring all kinds of compliments about his housekeeper's home-made lasagne.

'A really lovely woman in a nearby Italian store taught me how to make fresh pasta!' she was telling him proudly.

'What, here? In cynical old New York City?' joked Seamus.

'Tara has a particular naïve charm all of her own,' said Lucas coolly, and he couldn't miss the look of fury she directed at him as she brought out the tiramisu.

Eventually they all went home and Lucas tried to ignore the sound of Brett asking Tara for her email address. And it wasn't until Seamus and Erin had extracted a promise that the housekeeper would attend a ceilidh at the embassy that they finally took their leave.

The apartment seemed very big and very quiet as Lucas walked back into the library and found Tara clearing away glasses. 'Did you give Brett your email address?' he demanded.

'And if I did? Is that such a crime?' She straightened up to look at him and he had never seen such a look of quiet fury in her eyes. 'Unless you think...' She shook her head as if in disbelief. 'Unless you really think that I would encourage one man in a romantic fashion, when I'm in a physical relationship with another?'

Physical relationship. He didn't like the sound of that, but he supposed he couldn't doubt its accuracy. 'You were sending out all kinds of mixed messages tonight.'

'That's all in your head,' she retorted, bending towards the table once more. 'I was being friendly, that's all.'

'Leave that,' he said as she resumed putting crystal glasses onto a tray with such force he was surprised they didn't shatter.

'I'd rather do it now than in the morning.'

'I don't care—'

'No,' she interrupted suddenly and this time when she straightened up, the quiet fury in her eyes had been replaced with something stronger—something which blazed like fire. 'You couldn't have made that more plain if you'd tried! But maybe I'm fed up with the Lucas Conway approach to staff management! You taught me to cook something other than pie so I would be worthy of catering for your fancy guests and I ticked that off the list, didn't I? Then you decided to dress me up like one of those paper dolls you find in a child's magazine—and I went along with that, too. Heaven forbid that I should look like some screwball! But you're still not satisfied, are you, Lucas? And nothing ever *will* satisfy you, because basically you don't know yourself and you have no desire to learn about yourself, because you're a coward.'

The room went very silent. 'Excuse me?' he questioned, his words like ice. 'Did you just call me a coward?'

'You heard exactly what I said.'

Tara met his stony gaze and couldn't quite believe she'd done it but she couldn't back out now, no matter what the repercussions might be. Because she loved him and she wanted him to stop running away from his past— even if that meant the end of what the two of them shared. And even if it was, would that really be such a great loss? You couldn't really share anything with a man with no emotions, could you? A man who resolutely refused to allow himself to *feel* stuff.

'You can't live properly until you reconcile yourself with your past—and I don't think I can carry on like this until you do,' she breathed. 'Maybe you don't have any living blood relatives, but isn't that something which warrants a little investigation? Don't you want to know why your mother sold you? To find out who your real father is and whether either of them are alive? To discover whether she had any more children and if you have any brothers or sisters?' Her face suddenly crumpled. 'I know that when I—'

'No!' Furiously, he cut across her—the slicing wave of his hand a gesture of finality. 'I'm done with confessionals and I certainly don't want to waste any more of my evening listening to you, while you start unburdening your soul. To be honest, I'm tired, and I'm bored. I don't know how many times I've told you that I never wanted that kind of relationship and unless you can accept that, then I agree— we have no kind of future. So perhaps you might like to think about that. And now, if you'll excuse me—I'm going to bed. I'll see you in the morning.'

Tara's heart was pounding with shock as he turned and walked out of the library without another word. She could hear his footsteps going upstairs, along the corridor towards the master bedroom, and just for a moment she actually considered following him, until she drew herself up short.

Was she completely *insane*? He might as well have taken out a full-page ad in *The Washington Post*, saying, *Leave me alone*.

He'd told her he'd see her in the morning, and he'd done it with that cold and condemning look in his eyes. That wasn't the action of a man who wanted to cuddle and make up—that was a man who had been pushed to his limits. He was angry with her—but not nearly as angry as she was with herself. How long was she planning to hang around and get treated like someone who didn't really matter? Because she *did* matter. Not just for her baby's sake, but for her own.

She crept along to the second bedroom, uncomfortably aware that this was only the second night they'd spent apart since they'd resumed their sexual relationship—and she thought how big and lonely the bed seemed without him. Predictably, sleep was a long time in coming and when it did, dawn was just beginning to edge into the sky because she hadn't bothered to close the drapes.

When she awoke, the apartment was completely silent and, quickly, she got out of bed, wandering from room to room looking for Lucas, knowing with a sinking sense of certainty that she wasn't going to see him. The lingering aroma of coffee and some juiced halves of orange were the only signs of his presence. He must have had breakfast and then left. She looked around to see if there was a note, but of course there wasn't. And a huge pang of stupid longing swept over her as she tried to imagine what it would be like if he *was* the kind of man who left little messages dotted around the place. Affectionate words or cartoons, scribbled onto Post-it notes and stuck to the front of the refrigerator or left lying on a pillow. But those things only happened in films. or between real-life couples who genuinely loved one another. He'd only ever left her a note once before—when he'd brought forward his New York trip after they'd slept together and he'd told her he'd give her a good reference!

Back then he couldn't wait to get away from her and she wouldn't be here now if that night hadn't produced a child. Lucas would have moved on. And so would she. She'd have found herself a job as housekeeper to someone else and would now be throwing herself enthusiastically into her new role. Perhaps the discovery that she could enjoy sex might have provided some hope for the future— making her wonder if one day she'd be able to enjoy dating men who were more suitable than Lucas Conway.

Her stomach turned over at the thought

of being held in any other arms than his. It made her feel violently sick to think of any lover other than Lucas and the longer she allowed this situation to continue, the harder it was going to be to ever give him up. Because that time would come, most definitely—as surely as the sun rose over Manhattan each morning. They'd already had their first serious row and they'd both said some pretty wounding things. Maybe she should be grateful for his honesty. At least he wasn't encouraging her to build fanciful daydreams and maybe it was time she stopped trying to pretend that this relationship of theirs was going anywhere. Surely it would be better— for both of them—if they re-established the boundaries and negotiated a different kind of future. She swallowed, knowing that the only way to do that was to put distance between them.

For her to go home to Ireland. Back to where she belonged.

She cleared up the debris from the dinner party, then went into the en-suite wet room and stood beneath the cascading shower, trying to enjoy the moment, but the luxury products were wasted on her. She took extra time washing and drying her hair and even more time selecting what to wear. Which clothes to take and which to leave behind. She stared a little wistfully at the chiffon skirt and lace insert shoes; the silky dresses and impossibly fine cashmere sweaters. She loved those clothes—loved the way they made her feel— but they had no place in the life she was about to resume. So she took the shiny anorak, the jeans, the darker of the sweaters, the warmest dresses-as well as all of the underwear. Then she called a cab and checked she had money and her passport. It was only as she was leaving that she realised she couldn't just *go*— not without saying something. So she went slowly into the library where she picked up a pen and, with a heavy heart, began to write.

Lucas stared down at the note and a flare of something which felt close to pain clenched at his heart. But it wasn't pain, he told himself furiously. It was disappointment. Yes, that was it. Disappointment that Tara Fitzpatrick had just done a runner like some thief in the night. And after everything he'd done for her…

He tugged his cell-phone from his pocket and jabbed his finger against her number. It rang for so long that he thought it was going to voicemail, but then she picked it up and he heard that sweetly soft Irish brogue.

'Hello?'

'You're at the airport, I assume?' he clipped out.

'I am. I've managed to get the last seat on a flight which is leaving for Dublin in…' there was a rustle as, presumably, she lifted her arm to look at her watch '…twenty minutes' time.'

'So you're running out on me,' he said coldly. 'Without even bothering to tell me you were going. Now who's the coward, Tara?'

'No, Lucas,' she corrected. 'The cowardly thing to have done would be not to have picked up this call.'

He could feel control slipping away from him and he didn't like it, because hadn't his legendary control allowed him to make his world manageable? Hadn't taking command enabled him to rise, phoenix-like, from the ashes of his upbringing and forge himself a successful life? 'Why didn't you at least wait around until I was back from my meeting when we could have discussed this calmly, like grown-ups?' he demanded.

He heard a fractured sound, as if she was having difficulty slowing down her suddenly rapid breathing. But when she spoke she sounded calm and distant. Very distant. He frowned. And not like Tara at all.

'You once left me a note when you couldn't face having an important conversation with me. Do you remember that, Lucas? Well, it's my turn now—and I'm doing it for exactly the same reasons. I didn't want a protracted goodbye, nor to have to offer explanations, or listen to any more accusations. I don't want bitter words to rattle around in my brain and imprint themselves on my memory, when we need to keep this civilised. So I'll be in touch when I'm settled and you can see as much or as little of our baby as you want. That's all.' She drew in a deep breath before letting it out in a husky sigh. 'Don't you understand? I'm setting you free, Lucas.'

Something swelled up inside him like a growing wave—something dark and unwanted. How *dared* she offer him his freedom, when it was not hers to give? Did she consider him as some kind of puppet whose strings she could tug whenever the mood took her—just because she carried a part of him deep inside her? The dark feeling grew but deliberately he quashed it, because he needed to think clearly—his mind unobstructed by neither anger nor regret. Because maybe she was right. Maybe it *was* better this way. Better she left when things were tolerably amicable between them. Time and space would do the rest and once the dust had settled on their impetuous affair, they would be able to work out some kind of long-term plan. He would be good to her. That was a given. He would provide her with the finest home money could buy and all the childcare she needed. And he would...

He swallowed, wondering why his throat felt as if it had been lined with barbed wire which had been left out in the rain. Even if fatherhood was an unknown and an unwanted concept—that didn't mean he wasn't going to step up to the plate and be dutiful, did it? To be there for his child as his own father had never been there for him.

And if he found that impossible?

Why *wouldn't* he find it impossible, when he had no real template for family life? And wouldn't it then follow that he was probably going to let her and the baby down, somewhere along the line?

He swallowed as Tara's accusations came back to ring with silent reproach in his ears.

'Don't you want to know why your mother sold you? To find out who your real father is

and whether either of them are alive? To discover whether she had any more children?'

His mouth hardened. No, he didn't want to know any of those things. Why should he? In an ideal world he would have gone back to the life he'd had before. The one with no surprises. No analysis. No whip-slim woman challenging him with those sleepy amber eyes. But it wasn't that simple. Nothing ever was.

He cleared his throat. 'Just let me know when you get back to Dalkey,' he said coolly. 'And please keep me up to speed with your plans. I will return to Ireland in time for the birth.'

CHAPTER TWELVE

RAIN LASHED LOUDLY against the window and a gale howled like some malevolent monster in the dark night. In the distance Tara could hear trees creaking and the yelp of a frightened dog. She rolled over and shivered beneath the duvet, trying to breathe deeply, and, when that didn't work, to count backwards from one hundred. Anything, really, which would bring the oblivion and ease she craved in the form of sleep, if only for a few hours.

Because it was hard. She wasn't going to lie. If this was what being in love was like, then she wanted it out of her system as quickly as possible. The pain was unbearable. Pain like she'd never known. As if someone were inserting a burning poker into each ventricle of her heart. And the torture wasn't just causing physical pain—it was mental too, because the memory of Lucas was never far from her mind. It hovered in the background of her thoughts throughout every second of the day. The knowledge that he was no longer part of her life was like a heavy weight pressing down on her shoulders, so that most of the time she felt weary, even when she shouldn't have done.

She missed his face, his body, his banter. She missed being in his arms at night, wrapped in all that warm and powerful strength as he made love to her, over and over again. Angrily, she clenched her hands into two white-knuckled fists. Because that was a ridiculously romantic interpretation of what had taken place. They'd had amazing and exquisite sex, that was all, and presumably that was what he did with all the other women who had shared his bed—which perhaps made their dogged pursuit of him more understandable. She was the one who had elevated it to a level which was never intended, with her fanciful words of *love*. And in doing that, hadn't she followed the path of so many foolish women before her—her mother and her grandmother included? For the first time in her life, she acknowledged that Granny might have had a point in her often expressed and jaundiced view about men, as she'd waved her stick angrily in the air.

'I tell you, they're not worth it, Tara! Not a single one of them!'

But, outwardly at least, Tara was determined to present a positive face to the world. She made sure she looked after herself—exercising sensibly, eating regularly and faithfully keeping all her appointments at the hospital, who pronounced themselves delighted with her progress. She even continued to dress in the new style which had been shown to her so comprehensively in New York. She liked the way the new clothes made her feel. She liked the soft whisper of silk and cashmere against her skin and she liked wearing trousers which actually fitted her, rather than flapping around her legs. If she'd learnt one thing it was that her body was nothing to be ashamed of and that there was nothing wrong with wanting to take care of her appearance.

It was only at night, under the forgiving cloak of darkness, that she cried big salty tears which rolled down her cheeks and fell silently into her sodden pillow. That she ached to feel Lucas beside her again, even though in her heart she knew that was never going to happen. And each morning she awoke to sombre grey Dublin skies, which seemed to echo the bleakness of her mood.

But she was strong and she was resilient, and, once she'd adjusted to her new life, things began to improve. Or rather, once she'd accepted that Lucas wasn't going to suddenly turn up and sweep her off her feet—that was the turning point. She knew then she had to embrace the future, not keep wishing for something which was never going to happen. There was to be no fairy-tale ending. Lucas wasn't going to suddenly appear on the doorstep, his face obscured by a bouquet of flowers with a diamond ring hidden in his pocket. He'd told her he would be back for the birth—which was still four whole months away—which gave her plenty of time to erase him from her aching heart.

Aware that his Dalkey house held too many poignant memories, she began to bombard local employment agencies with her CV and quickly found a job—though not, as originally planned, in a big, noisy family. With a baby of her own on the way, she decided it was better to keep focussed on that. Her new position was as housekeeper to a couple of academics, in their big house overlooking Caragh Lake, in beautiful County Kerry.

Dana and Jim Doyle had both sat in on her interview, where Tara had been completely upfront about her situation.

'I'm pregnant and no longer with the father of my child. I don't know if that's going to be a problem for you,' she'd blurted out, 'but he is providing generous financial support for us both.'

'So do you really *need* to work?' Dana had asked gently.

'No, but I've always worked.' Tara's reply had been simple. She was unable to imagine the long days stretching ahead without some kind of structure to them, terrified of all those hours which could be devoted to pining for a man who didn't want her.

How long before she stopped feeling this way? Before her body stopped craving his touch and her lips his kiss?

She emailed Lucas her new address and he sent an instant response, asking if she had everything she needed. The answer to that was obviously no and yet, for some reason, the question infuriated her. Why did people keep asking her what she *needed* when she had a warm bed, a roof over her head, and a secure job, which was a lot more than many people had? Her needs weren't the problem but her wants were.

She stared into the mirror.

She still wanted Lucas—wasn't that the most agonising thing of all?

Her hand moving down to her growing bump, she told herself that these feelings would fade. They *had* to fade—because everything did eventually. The bullying at school—once unendurable—had leached from her consciousness once she'd left Ballykenna. Even the reason for that bullying—all the shame surrounding her ancestry—had receded, so that she hardly thought about it any more. And that had come about because she'd made a determined effort to erase it from her mind.

So do that now, with Lucas, or you'll spend the rest of your life as a ghost of a person, longing for something which can never be yours.

Tara bit her lip.

He was the father of her child. Nothing else.

Her mouth firmed.

Nothing.

As he was driven through the sweeping Argentinian landscape, Lucas felt the pounding of his heart. It was pounding like an out-of-control speed train. As he got out of the car he became aware that his mouth was dry and recognised that this was the closest he'd ever come to fear. Or maybe it was just apprehension. Glancing up at the big sign which read Sabato School of Polo, he took a moment to realise that someone must have heard the sound of his car and a man was walking towards him.

The man's build was much like his own—long-legged, strong and muscular—though the thick tumble of dark hair was distinctly longer. He wore casual riding clothes and leather boots which were dull with dust—an outfit which was in marked contrast to Lucas's own bespoke linen suit. But as he grew closer, Lucas found himself staring into a pair of dark-lashed and slanting green eyes, so unnervingly like his, as were the chiselled jaw and high slash of cheekbones.

And now the pounding of his heart became deafening as he acknowledged who it was who stood before him. His older brother. He swallowed. His only brother. For a moment neither man said anything, just stared long and hard, their faces set and serious. Two powerful tycoons confronted by the bitter reality of their past, which had somehow merged into the present.

'Alejandro,' said Lucas eventually.

The man nodded. 'I've spent a long time trying to find you, Lucas,' he breathed slowly.

And that was the main difference between them, Lucas acknowledged. That his brother's deep voice was accented, its lilting cadence emphasising the Spanish of his mother tongue. Lucas felt his heart clench, realising that his brother had known their real mother, while he had not, and he felt a bitter pang he hadn't expected before replying to his brother's statement. 'I changed my name,' he said, at last.

Alej nodded and then smiled, expelling a long sigh of something which sounded like relief. 'Want to tell me about it? Over a beer maybe, or even a ride? I don't even know if you ride—how crazy is that?'

For the first time Lucas smiled as he chose the latter option, even though he hadn't been on a horse in a while and even though his brother was an ex-world-champion polo player who could outride most people. But for once, he wasn't feeling competitive and he didn't care if Alej outshone him in the saddle. He wanted clarity in which to confront the past—not alcohol clouding or distorting the things which needed to be said. He wanted to hear the facts as they were, no matter how much they might hurt.

And they did hurt. No two ways about it. He had thought he was prepared for the pain which might be awaiting him when he heard the full story of how he came to be adopted, but afterwards wondered if perhaps he'd been naïve. Because was anyone ever really *prepared* for pain? Intellectually you might think you knew what to expect, but on a visceral level it always hit you with a force which could leave you breathless.

Hacking out over the lush green pastures, they rode for a long time, sometimes talking, sometimes lapsing into thoughtful silences, until the sinking sun had begun to splash the landscape with coral and Alej turned to him.

'You must be thirsty by now. Think it's time for that beer?'

Lucas nodded. 'Sure do.'

As if by unspoken consent, they urged their mounts into a fierce gallop as they headed back towards the stables and Lucas was glad for the sudden rush of adrenalin which surged through his veins. Glad too that the rush of air dried the tears he could feel on his cheeks.

His brother's car was waiting to take them to Alej's *estancia*, where his wife Emily was waiting with their baby Luis, and Lucas stepped into the warm family home and felt a rush of something he'd never experienced before. Was it envy or regret? he wondered. Because as Alej lifted the squealing Luis high in the air and the beautiful Emily stirred something in a pot which smelt delicious, Lucas realised that he too could have had this. A home and a family. With Tara. The woman who had encouraged him to come here. Who had made him dare raise the curtain on his past and look directly into the face of his brother and his troubled ancestry.

He swallowed as Emily handed him a frosted bottle of beer.

He could have had all this.

And he had blown it.

He didn't sleep well that night, even though the bed was supremely comfortable and the steak which Alej cooked for dinner the best he'd ever eaten, especially as it had been served with Emily's delicious spicy vegetables. But in the days which followed, he was given a tantalising taste of the country of his birth. He grew to understand it a little and to like it enormously so that by the time it came to leave, he experienced a distinct pang as he dropped a kiss on the baby's downy head and hugged Emily goodbye. He didn't say much as Alej drove him to the airport. He didn't need to. He knew that something powerful had been forged between the two of them during the past week, a bond which had been severed so many years ago but which had somehow, miraculously, endured.

At the airport the two men embraced. Then Lucas took one last look at the sweeping mountains he could see in the distance and, somewhere in his heart, knew he'd be back. 'You know, you and the family must visit me in Ireland.'

'*Por supuesto.*'

Once again their gazes clashed with the sense of something unspoken. And then he was in the aircraft and clipping his seat belt before the private jet barrelled along the runway and soared up into the cloudless sky. For a while Lucas stared down at the retreating rooftops of Buenos Aires, before settling back in his seat.

It was a long flight but for once he couldn't concentrate on work matters—even though he was able to communicate with his assistant on the ground. And somewhat predictably, when the plane touched down in Dublin, it was to a grey and blustery day. He thought how tiny Ireland seemed in comparison to the sweeping landscape of the country he'd just left. A pulse was beating at his temple as he stared down at the email his assistant had sent him earlier and, slowly, he gave his driver the address. All during the car journey to Caragh Lake, Lucas was aware of the racing of his heart and sudden clamminess of his palms—as if his body were trying to keep him focussed on what his mind was trying so hard to resist. But the dark thoughts kept flapping back, like insistent crows.

What if he couldn't do this?

What if she didn't want him? Could he blame her if she didn't? His mouth hardened. And mightn't that be best? Wouldn't that guarantee her some kind of peace, even if peace was a concept he couldn't ever imagine finding for himself? Not now, anyway.

Despite its size, the big house wasn't easy to find, tucked away in a leafy lane and overlooking a beautiful lake. As Lucas lifted the heavy door knocker he could hear it echoing through the large house and it seemed to take for ever before he heard the approach of oddly familiar footsteps, and when the door opened he saw Tara standing there. His heart leapt. The new Tara. The one with the feathery soft hair which made her look so sleek.

She was blinking at him in disbelief. 'Lucas?'

He heard the strangled note in her voice but of far more concern was the sudden blanching of her skin and the way her eyes had widened. Because there was no welcome in their amber depths and no smile on her soft lips. And her next words compounded his thumping fears.

'What are you doing here?' she demanded.

'Isn't it obvious? I've come here to see you.'

'And now you have. See? And I'm fine.'

She went to push the door shut again but he held up the palm of his hand.

'Tara.' His voice softened. 'That's not what I meant and you know it.'

Her face had lost none of its suspicion. 'You didn't warn me you were coming.'

'I thought unannounced was better.'

'Better? Better for who? Yourself, of course—because that's the only person you ever think about, isn't it?' Her voice rose. 'Are you crazy, Lucas? Didn't you think it mightn't be suitable for you to just come *barging* in like this? I might have been cooking lunch for Mr and Mrs Doyle.'

He didn't feel it prudent to point out that he'd had one of his assistants find out when her bosses were attending a conference on marine science in Sweden, and had timed his flight to Ireland accordingly. 'And are you allowed no life of your own?' he questioned archly.

The corners of her unsmiling mouth lifted but not with a smile—more like a rueful acknowledgement of some grim fact. 'You're probably better qualified than anyone to answer that question, Lucas. But that's beside the point. Why are you here?' She sucked in a deep breath, her hand leaning on the door jamb. 'Why are you here when you told me that you'd be back in time for the birth and that's still sixteen weeks away, by Dr Foley's reckoning.'

For the first time Lucas allowed his gaze to move from her face to her body and he was unprepared for the savage jolting of his heart. She looked…

His throat grew dry. He'd never really understood the description 'blooming' when applied to a pregnant woman, mainly because such a field was outside his area of interest. But he understood it now. She was wearing an apron covering a woollen dress of apple-green, and he could see that her slender frame had filled out. There was more flesh on her bones and her cheeks were fuller and, if he ignored the faint hostility in her gaze—which wasn't easy—he could see a radiance about her which seemed to make her glow from within. But it was the curve of her belly which made his heart begin to race.

Hesitation was something unfamiliar to him but he could sense he needed to be careful about what he said next—more careful than he'd ever been in his life—because she was still prickling with hostility. 'I'm here because I need to speak to you. To tell you things that perhaps you need to hear.'

Tara flinched, trying to put a lid on the rush of emotion which was flowing through her body. Because this wasn't fair. He'd told her he would see her for the birth, which was months away—precious months when she was supposed to be practising immunity when it came to looking into his beautiful face, that shadowed jaw and those emerald-bright eyes.

But she couldn't tell him that, could she? If she hinted that she couldn't cope with an unexpected visit from him, then wouldn't that make her appear weak?

She had no idea what he was about to say since she hadn't heard very much from him since she'd left America. For all she knew he might be about to announce that he'd finally met the love of his life, despite having vowed that he didn't *do* love. But stranger things had happened and some gorgeous New Yorker might have possessed just the right combination of beauty and dynamism to capture the billionaire's elusive heart.

And if that were the case, then wasn't it better to get it over with?

'You'd better come in,' she said grudgingly.

She was achingly aware of his presence as he followed her into the hallway, wishing her thoughts didn't keep going back to that first night, when it had all started. If only you could rewrite the past. If, say, she hadn't let Charlotte in that day, then none of this might ever have happened. But you couldn't rewrite the past and, anyway, would she really want to go back to the Tara she'd been back then? The unfulfilled misfit of a woman who'd never known real pleasure? And yes, the flip side to pleasure was emotional pain— unbearable pain for quite a while now—but you learnt through such experiences, didn't you? You learnt to cope and you became stronger—strong enough to handle an un-scheduled visit from the man whose child you carried.

'Would you like coffee?' she questioned, expecting him to say no.

But Lucas never did what you expected him to do.

'Actually, I would. I've missed your coffee, Tara.'

'I don't want any of your old flannel.'

His gaze was cool and unabashed. 'It isn't flannel. I'm merely stating a fact. Though they brew some pretty amazing stuff in Argentina.'

She blinked. 'Argentina?'

'Why don't you make the coffee first?' he said gently. 'And then we'll talk.'

Her instinctive fury at his reversion to the dominant role was supplanted by a natural curiosity but, grateful for the chance to get away from the distraction of that piercing green gaze, Tara hurried from the room. She returned minutes later, hating herself for having first checked her appearance in the kitchen mirror, because it wasn't as if she wanted to impress him, was it?

He was standing with his back to her, looking down over the sweeping emerald lawn and, beyond that, the darker green of the trees, through which you could see the silver glimmer of the lake and, fringing those, the gentle hills of Ireland. Something poignant shafted at Tara's heart but she forced herself to suppress it, because she needed to keep calm.

He turned to face her and she could feel an annoying shiver of awareness but she quashed it. With a hostess-like air, she indicated that he should sit down and watched as he lowered his powerful frame into one of the worn velvet seats which the non-materialistic Dana Doyle had told her they'd had for years. And when she'd given him his coffee, just the way he liked it, Tara perched on a more upright chair opposite, not quite trusting her trembling fingers to hold the water she'd poured for herself.

'So,' she said, with a tight smile. 'What is it that you want to speak to me about, Lucas?'

She was unprepared for the sudden darkness which crossed his rugged features, like a black cloud suddenly obscuring the face of the moon. And for a look of something she'd never seen in his eyes before, something which on anyone else she might have described as desolation. But Lucas didn't do desolation and she wasn't here to analyse his moods or to try to get inside his head. This was a matter-of-fact meeting and he probably wanted to discuss financial support for her and the baby.

He stared down at the inky brew in his cup and put it down untasted, before lifting his gaze to hers.

'I took your advice,' he said simply. 'And went to Argentina.'

CHAPTER THIRTEEN

'YOU WENT TO ARGENTINA,' Tara repeated slowly.

He nodded. 'I did.'

There was a momentary pause. 'And what did you find there, Lucas?'

She was staring deep into his eyes, her expression as distant as ever he'd seen it, and Lucas wondered if coming here unannounced had been a crazy idea. But he owed her this. He owed her the knowledge which had first shocked and then saddened him. And he owed it to himself to discover whether he had messed everything up.

'I found my brother there,' he said simply.

'You have a brother?'

'I do. His name is Alej—Alejandro Sabato— and he has a family of his own. His wife is English and she's called Emily and they have a young baby, Luis.'

'That's nice,' she said stiffly.

He wanted to tell her about the terrible pain in his heart because he'd missed her so much, but old habits died hard and for the time being he sought refuge in facts. 'He'd actually been trying to find me, but because I'd changed my name his investigators kept coming up with blanks. Anyway, he was able to fill me in on everything I needed to know.'

Her gaze was still steady. 'Which is?'

He shrugged his shoulders, for there was no easy way to say this, no acceptable way of defining the harsh facts surrounding his conception. 'My mother was a prostitute and my father was one of her clients,' he bit out. 'A drunken thief who used to spend long periods in prison, and when he was released he would come out, beat her up and make her pregnant.'

She licked her lips and he could see a swallowing movement in her throat. 'So how did you come—?'

'To be brought up in one of the most expensive parts of one of the most expensive cities in the world?' he supplied, and she nodded. 'My mother had given birth to Alej just a year earlier and she was having enough trouble feeding one child, let alone another. So she decided to sell me. I suppose it made perfect economic sense. She went to see someone in Buenos Aires—someone who put her in touch with a rich American heiress—'

'Your mother?' she interrupted breathlessly.

'No!' he negated viciously. 'Wanda Gonzalez never earned the right to call herself that during her lifetime, so I'm damned sure I'm not going to honour her with that title now she's dead.' He gave a bitter laugh. 'She had specified that she wanted a birth mother from Argentina, so that I would resemble my "father" as much as possible.'

'And did you?' she questioned curiously. 'Resemble him, I mean?'

He shook his head. 'Not really. We had the same hair colour, but that was about it—I was bigger, stronger, more powerful.' He gave a short laugh. 'And that's how I came to be brought up amid such great wealth in Manhattan, while Alejandro lived a very different life in Argentina—that is, until he escaped from abject poverty to become one of the world's greatest polo players.'

'Alejandro Sabato,' she ventured slowly, with a nod of her flame-bright hair. 'Yes, I've heard of him.'

'I'm sure you have. He was a bit of a poster-boy for the sport in his time. But I haven't come here to talk about my brother, Tara.'

She became instantly alert. 'No?' she challenged.

He wanted her to make this easy for him. To soften her lips into a smile. To send him a soft, unspoken message with her eyes so he could get up and walk right over there. Pull her hungrily into his arms and kiss her as he'd dreamt of doing ever since she'd walked out of his New York apartment. Because if he started kissing her and they began to make love, surely it would blot away some of the pain.

But something stopped him and it was the sense that this was the biggest deal he'd ever tried to pull off and he couldn't afford to get it wrong. Yet getting it wrong was a distinct possibility, even though he knew how to wheel and deal in a boardroom. When to talk and when to let silence work for you. He knew about joint venture capital, about leasing out cars or lorries which people couldn't afford to buy themselves, but he knew nothing about telling a woman that he loved her. And wasn't that the crux of what he really wanted to say to her? The most important thing.

No. First up he needed to acknowledge what she had done for him. To tell her some of the things he had felt. Still felt. 'I wanted to be angry with my mother and to blame her for the life into which I was born,' he whispered. 'And for a while I was. But then I realised that she'd taken a bad situation and tried to make it better. It can't have been easy to give me away, but she did. And she did it for me, so I wouldn't starve—and so that Alej wouldn't starve either. She probably thought she was giving me the best chance she could—she wasn't to know that Wanda was weak and Diego was cruel.'

'Lucas,' she said, and for the first time he could hear a softening of her voice and saw concern pleating her brow, as if she had detected his pain and wanted to soothe it away.

But he shook his head to silence her because he needed to say it, to let it all out so it could no longer gnaw away at him.

'I would never have found this out if you hadn't encouraged me to find my brother,' he said. 'You are responsible for that, Tara. For the bond I now have with my brother. For the discovery that I have a nephew and a sister-in-law. But when I saw that family of theirs it was like a dagger to my heart.'

'Lucas!' she said, as if she could hardly believe he was saying stuff like this, and wasn't there a part of him who could hardly believe it himself?

'I realised then that I had been given the opportunity to have a loving family—with you,' he said huskily. 'And because of my pride and arrogance and my cold and unfeeling heart, I had probably blown it. But I'm hoping against hope that I haven't blown it and I'm asking you to give me another chance because... I love you, Tara.'

She was shaking her head as if she didn't believe it, but the brief clouding of her eyes told him she didn't *dare* believe it and he knew he wasn't in the clear yet.

'I love your spirit and the way you answer me back,' he continued softly, and his eyes crinkled. 'Even although sometimes that trait makes me as mad as hell. I like the way you're loyal and true and that beneath your often prickly exterior there beats a heart of pure gold.' He swallowed. 'The first time I made love to you, it was like nothing I'd ever experienced. The way you made me feel was completely alien to me—'

She pursed her lips together. 'That's why

you couldn't wait to dash away the next morning and fly to New York early?'

'Because it scared the hell out of me,' he admitted. 'It made me feel vulnerable, in a way I hadn't allowed myself to feel for years. And then, when I told you stuff I'd kept bottled up for so long and you comforted me with your arms and with your body...' He swallowed. 'You just rocked my world. You're still rocking it. Even now when I told you about my real mother and father, you just accepted it calmly. I was watching your face and you didn't seem appalled, or shocked. You didn't start expressing fears about what bad blood I may have being passed onto our baby.' He saw her flinch. 'Listen to me, Tara, I know I handled it badly but I didn't know at the time *how* to handle it. But now I do. I'm asking you to forgive me and telling you that since you've been gone my life seems empty. To tell you that I want to marry you and spend the rest of my life with you. To give our child love and security, as well as to each other. To create a family. A real family. The kind of family which neither of us has ever had before. That is...that is if you feel you could ever love me too. So what do you say, Tara Fitzpatrick?'

Right then Tara was finding it impossible to say *anything*, she was feeling so choked up. Because Lucas might not be carrying a big bunch of flowers and a diamond ring, but he *was* telling her he loved her and he was asking her to marry him.

But he still didn't know, did he?

He didn't know everything about her because she'd kept her own guilty little secrets. And although she'd tried several times to tell him about her past—hadn't she been quietly glad when he'd cut her short? Hadn't that given her the justification she'd needed to bury it even deeper—to act as if she were Tara Goody-Two-Shoes—in which case, perhaps *she* was the coward, after all.

'I'm not the woman you think I am,' she said slowly.

'You're everything—'

'No. I'm not. Hear me out, Lucas. Please. Because this is important.' She stood up, because it was difficult sitting there in the piercing green spotlight of his gaze. So she walked around the Doyles' lovely old sitting room, with its faded furniture and leaf-framed view over the silvery lake, and gave a small sigh as she began her story. 'My mother was a nurse in England when she got pregnant by someone whose name I was never told.' Her voice grew reflective. 'She never saw him again, so she came back to Ireland with me and I was brought up by my grandmother, while Mammy went out to work. We lived pretty much hand to mouth, in a little cottage on the outskirts of Ballykenna, and when I was two, my mother got breast cancer—'

'Tara.'

'No, Lucas,' she said fiercely. 'Let me finish. She got breast cancer and it was very aggressive. It was obviously very sad but I can't remember much about it, or maybe I just blocked it out. She died very quickly and I was left in the sole care of my grandmother.' She swallowed as she made an admission she'd never dared make before, even to herself. To realise that just because someone went through the mechanics of caring for you, didn't mean that they liked you or loved you. Especially if you reminded them of their own failings.

'She was a cold and bitter woman,' she continued, with a wince. 'Though it took me a long time to find out why. To discover why she hated men so much and why she used to dress me like a frump.' She swallowed. 'And why the other children used to laugh at me behind my back.'

'Why?'

She drew in a deep breath. Here it was. The truth—in all its unvarnished clarity. 'My grandmother had been a nun and my grandfather a priest and their liaison was a huge scandal at the time, because my mother was the result of that liaison. Oh, they tried to hush it up but everyone knew. And I think that some of the burden of the guilt my grandmother carried around with her must have transferred itself onto me. It's why I was terrified of men and of intimacy until I met you, Lucas.'

She didn't know what she expected him to do, but she'd imagined *some* moment of reflection while he processed what she'd just told him. As if he'd need time to come to terms with her revelation and maybe to get his head around what a massive scandal it had been at the time. But instead he was getting up out of the faded velvet chair and crossing the room with a purposefulness which was achingly familiar to her. And when he put his arms around her and pulled her close, she started to cry and once she had started she couldn't seem to stop. The tears came hard and fast and Tara realised she was crying for all kinds of reasons. She was crying for the women of earlier generations who'd had to deal with judgement and being shunned. And she was crying for her poor dead mother who would never know her grandchild. Those tears were of sorrow, but hot on their heels came tears of gratitude, and joy—for being fit and healthy and carrying a child beneath her fast-beating heart. A child who...

She turned her wet face up to Lucas and saw compassion and love blazing from his green eyes and that gave her the courage to tell him. 'I love you, Lucas,' she whispered. 'So much. And yes, I want to spend the rest of my life with you.'

He nodded, but didn't speak, just drew his arms around her even tighter and for now that was enough.

It was more than enough.

EPILOGUE

'Lucas…' Tara gave a luxurious stretch as she felt the warm lips of her husband tracking over her bare stomach, making her flesh shiver into little goosebumps. *Again.*

She swallowed down her growing desire, because they'd only just made love, hadn't they? Was it always going to be this good? she wondered dreamily.

'We'll…we'll be late for dinner.'

'Dinner isn't until nine-thirty,' he whispered. 'You know they eat late in Argentina.'

'Yes, but even so.' She fluttered her fingertips to his bare shoulders. 'We really ought to be getting dressed.'

'Say that with meaning, Tara.' There was a note of laughter in his voice as he moved to lie on top of her. 'And perhaps we will.'

Within minutes she was gasping out his name as he drove into her and he was kissing away the sounds of her helpless little cries as she came. But even though a deep lethargy crept over her afterwards, Tara forced herself to wriggle out from beneath Lucas's hard, honed flesh and head for the en-suite bathroom, because they had a whole delicious evening ahead of them. Quickly, she showered and, when Lucas took her place to stand beneath the powering jets, she returned to the bedroom to slither into a silky black jersey dress and matching pumps, before creeping along the corridor to where Declan was fast asleep, in a cot beside his bigger cousin, Luis.

For a moment she just stood there, gazing down at the dark heads of the two sleeping babes, and a great wave of love and contentment swelled up inside her. They were so lucky, she thought, with a sudden twist of her heart. So very lucky. All of them.

She and Lucas had been married in Dublin just before the birth of their beloved son, Declan. Her friend Stella had been bridesmaid and the celebrations had been memorable for many reasons, not least because Stella had rebuffed the advances of the Italian billionaire Salvatore di Luca, which was pretty much unheard of. And the guest of honour had been Brett Henderson—the actor who had caused

Lucas to be so jealous in New York—who had offered to sing a song at their wedding, about love changing everything.

'He's clearly still smitten,' Lucas had grumbled, when she'd excitedly shown him the email.

'Rubbish,' Tara had disagreed. 'I think he just likes a woman with an Irish accent—in which case he'll have plenty to choose from at the reception! Our friends will never forgive us if we say no, Lucas. And besides, nobody could disagree with the sentiments of the song he's planning to sing, could they?'

And Lucas had no answer to that.

Their honeymoon had been postponed until Declan was six months old, when they went on an extended stay with Alej, Emily and Luis at their beautiful Argentinian *estancia*. The two women had hit it off immediately and it had warmed Tara's heart to see Lucas bonding with the brother he was quickly getting to know. Her husband was learning about the land of his birth, too, and had changed his name back to his birth name—not the one he'd seen written above a pub on the very first night he'd arrived in Dublin, completely alone. As Lucas Sabato he was building a mother-and-baby unit outside Buenos

Aires, to support women and children who had fallen on hard times. Tara swallowed. To help prevent another helpless baby being given up because his mother couldn't afford to feed him…

And tonight they would eat outside beneath the stars with Emily and Alej and count every single one of their blessings.

She heard soft footsteps behind her and felt the whisper of Lucas's lips against her neck. His arm snaked around her waist and for a moment the two of them were silent as they stood looking down at their son.

'It's crazy,' said Lucas softly.

'What is?'

He shrugged. 'How I've gone from being a man with nothing to a man who has everything.'

She turned to look at him, an expression of bemusement on her face. 'Some people wouldn't describe a relatively young billionaire as a man with nothing.'

He shook his head. 'All the money in the world doesn't come close to the way I feel when I look at you, and Declan. Because you have given me all that is properly precious. You gave me courage to seek out my family and doing that has enriched my life. You have given me a beautiful son. But most of all, you've given me your love and that is priceless.' He tilted her chin, his voice a little unsteady. 'You are my everything, Tara Sabato, do you realise that?'

He had taken her breath away with his soft words and Tara had to dab furiously at her eyes to stop her mascara running. 'And you are my everything,' she answered fiercely. 'For the first time in my life I feel as if I have a real home and that you and Declan are the beating heart of that home. And I love you. I love you so much. You do know that, don't you, Lucas?'

Tenderly, Lucas stared down into the amber gleam of her eyes. The woman he admired more than any other. Who was strong and smart and brave and beautiful. His equal. His wife. His love. 'Do I know that?' He smiled as he wiped a mascara-coloured teardrop away from her freckled cheek. 'You betcha.'

* * * * *

If you enjoyed
The Argentinian's Baby of Scandal
by Sharon Kendrick
look out for the first instalment in
The Legendary Argentinian Billionaires duet
Bought Bride for the Argentinian
available now!

And why not explore these other
One Night With Consequences stories?

Heiress's Pregnancy Scandal
by Julia James

Innocent's Nine-Month Scandal
by Dani Collins

Greek's Baby of Redemption
by Kate Hewitt

His Two Royal Secrets
by Caitlin Crews

Available now!